"Are you ~~...~~ Alexis, Dad?"

Judd raised an eyebrow in surprise. "Where did you pick up that phrase?"

"Andy. He said you have the hots for her."

"That boy is entirely too sophisticated as well as badly informed," Judd said wryly.

"You do like Alexis, though, right?" The hope in Bryan's voice was almost painful to hear.

Judd searched for the right words. "This is an opportunity for me to get to know her better, that's all. We're friends." He debated between the white shirt and the blue, wishing Bryan would stop tormenting him with his questions.

"Aren't you gonna kiss her?"

"Bryan, that's enough. Go get my navy jacket lying on the bed."

"Your *new* jacket? You *are* going to kiss her!" Bryan gave a whoop.

Judd closed his eyes and counted to ten.

These two award-winning North American authors travel
four hundred miles to write together. Each brings a wealth
of experience to their collaborative effort. **Pamela Bauer**
has written twenty romances, and **Judy Kaye** is the author
of fifty romance, young adult/children's fiction and
nonfiction titles. Collaborating comes so naturally they
think they might be sisters separated at birth. Each has
a tolerant husband, two children and a dog that thinks
it's human.

Books by Pamela Bauer & Judy Kaye

HARLEQUIN ROMANCE®
3485—A WIFE FOR CHRISTMAS
3506—ALMOST A FATHER

Don't miss any of our special offers. Write to us at the
following address for information on our newest releases.

Harlequin Reader Service
U.S.: 3010 Walden Ave., P.O. Box 1325, Buffalo, NY 14269
Canadian: P.O. Box 609, Fort Erie, Ont. L2A 5X3

Make-Believe Mother

Pamela Bauer & Judy Kaye

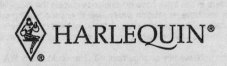

TORONTO • NEW YORK • LONDON
AMSTERDAM • PARIS • SYDNEY • HAMBURG
STOCKHOLM • ATHENS • TOKYO • MILAN • MADRID
PRAGUE • WARSAW • BUDAPEST • AUCKLAND

For Kathleen Eagle and Sandy Huseby, the two best
friends a writing team could have.
Viva the Prairie Writers Guild!

ISBN 0-373-03538-1

MAKE-BELIEVE MOTHER

First North American Publication 1999.

Copyright © 1998 by Pamela Bauer and Judy Kaye.

PROLOGUE

IT WAS five minutes to eight on a Friday night, and Bryan Shepard's father still wasn't home from work. Their housekeeper, Mrs. Wahlstrom, was in the kitchen talking on the phone. Some nine-year-olds might have felt neglected, but not Bryan. Actually, he was happy Mrs. Wahlstrom liked to talk on the phone and that his dad often worked late on Fridays because it meant he could watch "Two Plus Two" on television. His dad didn't like television very much, and the only reason they had one in the house at all was so that they could watch the news.

Bryan plumped a pillow and settled it behind him on the couch. Using the remote control, he channel surfed until the digital clock flashed eight o'clock. Then he turned to channel seven, and a familiar theme song began to play. A satisfied smile tweaked his lips as animated identical twin nine-year-old boys skateboarded across the screen. They were chased by their father, who zigzagged behind them, trying in vain to catch them. Finally, a tall, statuesque woman appeared, lassoing the three of them with a string of hearts.

As the cartoon introduction faded away, the opening scene of the sitcom revealed Katie Roberts, the

twins' mother, baking sugar cookies in the shapes of
cars. The boys were intently decorating them with
frosting and colorful sprinkles. The perfect mom,
Katie, smiled and praised them for their artistry.

Bryan sighed. Even though Mrs. Wahlstrom was a
nice enough lady and let him watch TV, she never
made cookies with him.

With each episode of "Two Plus Two" there was
a problem that needed to be solved. Tonight it involved a bully who was making life miserable for the
boys at school. Bryan immersed himself in the sitcom,
eager to find out how the twins' mom and dad would
solve the problem. They always solved the problems
together. They were a real family with a real mom—
something Bryan didn't have.

Katie Roberts was so cool. And so pretty. And
smart. Again, he sighed. If only he could have a mom
like her.

CHAPTER ONE

THE last place Judd Shepard wanted to be on a Saturday afternoon was at the mall. His son dragged him there, however, on the pretext of needing a new pair of jeans. When they arrived at the shopping center and Judd saw the line of kids threading through the corridor of shops, he suspected his son's desire had little to do with new clothes.

"Oh, look!" Bryan exclaimed with surprise as genuine as a three-dollar bill. "There are TV stars signing autographs today!"

Judd's eyes followed the serpentine line of youths to the center atrium, where a huge banner hung from the ceiling. It read, Ridgedale Mall Welcomes "Two Plus Two's" Katie Roberts.

"It looks like just one star to me," Judd commented dryly.

"It's Katie Roberts! Cool!" Bryan craned his neck to find the end of the line.

Judd tried to ignore his son's interest. "Let's try Mason's Department Store. They should have Levi's."

"Wait! Can't I get a picture, Dad? Huh? Please?" Bryan tugged on his father's arm and dragged the soles of his tennis shoes on the tiled floor.

7

Judd sighed. "We don't have time. I told Frankie I'd be back by four, and it's two-thirty now. I'm short one pilot today. I can't be away from the office long in case they need me to fly."

"We can be home in ten minutes if your beeper goes off," Bryan said logically. "Besides, Katie Roberts will never come back to our mall. I gotta get her autograph now. It might be my only chance!"

Judd grimaced at the desperation in his son's voice. His obsession with the TV program "Two Plus Two" was getting out of hand. Bryan didn't want to leave the house on Friday evenings because he was afraid he might not be home in time for the show. He'd cut photos of the TV family from magazines and pasted them on the walls of his bedroom. And lately he'd begun saying in a wistful fashion, "If Katie were my mom…"

"Come on, Dad. Please?"

If he hadn't looked like a puppy begging for affection, Judd might have been able to refuse. "Go on. Get in line. I'll catch up." He watched his dark-haired son race toward the mass of Katie fans and sighed. He hoped it was harmless, this long-distance infatuation with a TV mom.

It was certainly understandable. When Bryan's mother had died, their world had been turned upside down. He and Bryan had spent much of the last year looking for something to fill the void her death had left in their lives.

At least Judd had his work. Being owner and operator of an air ambulance service was a consuming occupation. There were times, in the midst of a critical transport, that he forgot everything but the task at hand. Working to help someone through a crisis held his emotions at bay. However, once he left his job, the loneliness, the sadness and the regret came flooding back.

But Bryan didn't have even that much reprieve. To Judd's dismay, his son often sought escape by watching television. Judd and his wife hadn't owned a television the first few years of their marriage. They'd read books, listened to music, danced barefoot on the carpet.

When Carol had given birth to Bryan, they had made a pact that television wouldn't play a major role in his life. She had been the one who monitored his viewing, making sure he only watched shows appropriate for a child and limiting the time he spent in front of the TV.

Since her death, Judd had found it difficult to stick to her plan. Because of his demanding work schedule, Bryan was often left with Mrs. Wahlstrom. Although the housekeeper had strict instructions, Judd knew that she didn't follow them. The older woman believed that to a small boy who had lost his mother, family programs such as "Two Plus Two" provided a comfort that was missing in Bryan's life. Because she was a great child-care provider in every other sense of the word, Judd overlooked the fact that she allowed Bryan this liberty.

Judd glanced at his watch and then at the line winding toward the table where the actress sat, signing black and white glossies and flashing her dazzling smile. Her hair was a sun-streaked honey-blond mane, her teeth an orthodontist's pride and her makeup flawless. She wore a tight-fitting sweater that emphasized her slender but curvy figure. She was, Judd concluded disinterestedly, as perfect and as plastic as every other starlet in Hollywood.

He fingered his beeper, hoping it wouldn't go off. He hadn't spent much time with Bryan lately and he missed that. As soon as they could get away from the autograph hounds, they'd buy the jeans and then get a milk shake.

Bryan was almost to the front of the line when he waved at his dad excitedly, motioning for him to join him. Reluctantly, Judd worked his way toward his son.

If there was one thing he could say for the actress, it was that she could sign her name very quickly. A few impersonal words, a smile meant to dazzle and a photograph shoved to the recipient by a publicity agent at her side. She had the act perfected.

Bryan wiggled anxiously, his cheeks rosy at the prospect of meeting a star from his favorite program. "She's really neat, isn't she, Dad?" he said reverently, staring at the blonde as if he were in a stupor.

Judd gave his son a nudge. "Move up. Your turn's coming."

Bryan's eyes widened, and he grinned unabashedly as the television star glanced at him.

"Hi, there. What's your name?" she asked, giving him the smile she had bestowed on the hundreds before him.

"Bryan. And this is my dad." He tugged on Judd's sleeve.

"Hi, Bryan's dad." She flashed the same smile at Judd, who felt an odd little catch in his chest when her green eyes met his. In an instant she had signed a photograph for Bryan, then asked Judd, "Would Dad like one, too?"

For the first time since Carol had died, Judd felt the stirrings of attraction. The look in the celebrity's eyes made him feel as if he were about to step off a cliff. The feeling was not a welcome one. Consequently, he was a bit harsh as he said, "No, Dad doesn't want one."

The only sign of emotion from the TV star was a delicate arch of one eyebrow. She flashed another smile at Bryan, then dismissed them by asking the next person in line what name she should put on the photo.

"Dad, you should have taken one. Then I could have had two!" Bryan grumbled as they walked away from the table.

"You don't need two," Judd said gruffly, his stride lengthening in an effort to get away from the celebrity and her provocative green eyes. Just then his beeper sounded. His time with Bryan was over, and all they had done was stand in line to see a Hollywood personality. Instead of getting the jeans and eating ice cream, they returned home. Mrs. Wahlstrom was summoned, and Judd hurried to the emergency demanding his attention.

It was late that night when he finally returned. Bryan was already in bed. Mrs. Wahlstrom had fallen asleep on the sofa. She awoke with a start when Judd closed the door.

"Oh! It must be late!" She patted her gray curls and straightened the skirt of her dress.

"I'm sorry. It took longer than I expected," Judd apologized.

"Do you realize how long I've been here, Mr. Shepard?"

It was the first time the older woman had approached the subject of his irregular hours. Judd sensed he was in for a dressing down. "I'll pay you double for the additional time, Mrs. Wahlstrom." He reached for his wallet, but she waved him off.

"I don't want extra money. I enjoy being with your son," she said sincerely. "It's Bryan I'm worried about. He shouldn't be spending so much time with an old lady like me."

"You're good for him, Mrs. Wahlstrom. And that's why I want to pay you a bonus." He tried again to give her some money, but she refused.

"I'm like a grandmother to him." She folded her arms across her ample bosom. "There's something I think you ought to know."

"What's that?"

"When he says his prayers before he goes to bed at night, he asks for a mother."

Judd felt as if someone had hit him in the stomach. "I didn't realize that." He rubbed a hand across the back of his neck. "It's probably all those TV sitcoms he watches. They all show these kids with ideal moms." He laughed sarcastically. "As if there's a woman out there who could be that perfect."

"I don't think he wants a perfect mother. Just someone to love him," Mrs. Wahlstrom remarked, then said good-night.

As soon as she was gone, Judd padded softly into Bryan's room. The night-light cast a golden glow about the boy's bed, giving him an angelic look. Everyone said he was a carbon copy of Judd, with his chestnut brown hair and angular features. Judd felt a surge of pride and bent to give him a kiss. As he did so, he noticed the eight-by-ten glossy of the "Two Plus Two" television mom hanging over the bed.

Judd stared at the picture, wishing his son wouldn't look for comfort to an actress who only pretended to be a loving, nurturing mother. "You're awfully good at captivating little boys, aren't you?" he whispered to the glossy photo. Judd would have ripped the picture from the wall, but he knew it wasn't necessary. She was only a TV personality. Bryan would never see her again. And eventually the sitcom would be canceled.

"Good night, Bry," Judd said softly, then tiptoed

out of the room. However, as he pulled the door shut it wasn't his son's face he saw, but the lovely Katie Roberts's, the perfect TV mom. As much as he hated to admit it, he understood exactly why his son was attracted to the woman.

"When's Dad coming home?"

Mrs. Wahlstrom frowned at Bryan over the rim of her glasses as she cleaned the silverware she'd discovered in a bottom cupboard. "He said he'd call, dear. I'm not a mind reader. Your father has very big responsibilities—saving people's lives, flying airplanes and helicopters, running a business. He can't be giving you an account of every minute of his day."

She pushed her glasses up her nose with the back of her hand. "Why don't you come and help me polish these forks? Look at how dark and dingy they are."

"Why are you cleaning them, anyway? Me and Dad don't invite people over for dinner. Not since Mom died. You're just wasting your time." Bryan slid off the couch.

"It's Dad and I, Bryan," she corrected him.

He shrugged. "Can I go to the ball park on Walnut and watch the high school team practice?"

"Too far away," Mrs. Wahlstrom said firmly. "No telling what kind of mischief you might get into there."

"Then I'll go to the convenience store and get

some baseball cards. Dad gave me money. Besides, that's two blocks closer.''

"They don't need a little boy hanging around, touching things,'' she retorted. "Anyway, those stores are a magnet for robberies. You wait for your father before you get those cards.''

Mrs. Wahlstrom was impossible today. When *was* his dad coming home?

"Then I'll go to church,'' Bryan retorted. "What trouble can I get into there?''

"Don't be smart with me, young man.'' She pointed her finger at him. "Find something to do.''

Bryan drifted to the window and stared at the driveway and lawn. As he was about to turn away, a moving van pulled into the complex and lumbered to a stop in front of the building.

"Somebody's moving in!'' Bryan announced delightedly. "A truck just came. Can I go watch them unload?''

Mrs. Wahlstrom looked as if she might say no, but to Bryan's surprise she answered, "All right, but be careful that you don't get in the way. And take a jacket.''

Bryan scurried out before she could saddle him with overshoes and a hat. Mrs. Wahlstrom just didn't understand boys.

"Hiya,'' Bryan greeted the two burly moving men. They had just opened the doors and were pulling a ramp into place between the truck and the ground.

"Hi, kid," one of them responded. "Do you know where apartment ten is?"

"Yup. It's right across from mine," Bryan answered. "You want me to show you?"

"Sure."

Bryan led the man inside. Lenny, the building superintendent, was already unlocking the door to the apartment when they arrived. He smiled at Bryan and greeted the mover.

"Miss Gordon called and said she'll be a little late," Lenny said. "She wants you to get started, since all the boxes are marked."

Bryan mulled over this tiny bit of information. The new neighbor was a she. That probably meant there was no husband—and no kids, either. A wave of disappointment washed over him. Kids never seemed to move into these apartments.

Bryan watched the first piece of furniture being carried inside. His eyes widened at the size of the gigantic television screen passing him. Next came a wall unit of enormous proportions. There were several boxes marked Video. This new neighbor was growing more interesting by the moment.

The rest of the furniture was pretty normal, Bryan decided. Frilly ruffled couches, a big brass bed with lots of curlicues and what one of the movers referred to as a makeup table. Bryan was on his way outside when a woman came down the hall toward him, her high-heeled shoes making no sound on the cushiony carpet.

Bryan looked at her and glanced away. Then, as his brain began to process what his eyes were seeing, his head spun and he stared openly. It was Katie Roberts—his favorite TV mom!

She was even more beautiful than he remembered, tall and slender, with hair the color of the honey he poured on his oatmeal in the morning. She wore a short dark skirt and a crisp white blouse much like the ones she often wore on "Two Plus Two."

Bryan was enthralled. She was the most beautiful mom in the world and she was moving into the apartment across the hall from him! His feet froze and his jaw locked open in dumbfounded delight.

"Hello, there." Her voice sounded the same as it did on TV and made his insides feel all squiggly.

"H-h-hullo," Bryan stammered, wondering if his brain, tongue and feet were connected. They must be, since they'd all stopped working at once.

Alexis Gordon smiled when she saw the small boy, mouth gaping, eyes wide as salad plates. She was accustomed to such adoration from young men—older ones, too. "Do you live here?"

Bryan nodded, pointing to his door.

"Then we'll be neighbors." Alexis surveyed the hall. "Are there many children in this building?"

"No, just me. Do you have any kids?" His eyes were hopeful.

"Uh-uh. No kids and no husband." Alexis wondered if the day would ever come when that would change. When she had left her small hometown in the mountains of Colorado, she had had one goal in mind—to make a living as an actress. Little did she know just how successful she would become or how difficult it would be to have a normal life as a celebrity. It hadn't taken long to discover that Hollywood was not the place to raise a family. A feeling of homesickness washed over her at the sight of this fresh-faced little boy, who reminded her of her younger brother, Timmy, and everything she had left behind in Colorado.

"Why?"

Alexis blinked. "What?"

"Why don't you have kids?" As if he suddenly realized the enormity of his impertinent question, he blushed. "I mean, you're such a great mom on TV that I thought you must have *lots* of children."

"Then you know who I am?"

He grinned shyly. "You're Katie."

"Actually, my name is Alexis. Alexis Gordon."

"I'm Bryan Shepard." He offered her his hand in an adult manner. "You really are a great mom, you know."

"Why, thank you." Alexis gave him her most motherly sitcom smile. "That was a very sweet thing to say."

"I've been helping the movers," Bryan announced, puffing up his small chest.

"Why, how thoughtful of you. Thank you very much," Alexis said sincerely.

"You have a lot of nice stuff." He peered through the open door. "I've never seen such a big TV."

Alexis could see that he wanted to come inside. There was something in the way he stood, looking shyly at her, his small shoulders slumped.

"Have you lived here long?" she asked.

"About a year. It's a pretty good place to live, but I liked our house better. I had more friends there. There aren't very many kids around here."

Which was why Alexis had chosen the complex. It wasn't that she disliked children, but she needed to be able to come home to a quiet building and not have to continue her role as Katie Roberts.

"And there's a lot of rules, too," he added.

There was a sadness in his eyes that tugged on Alexis's heartstrings. She wondered what had prompted Bryan's parents to move from a house to an apartment, but thought it would be better not to ask. Being a popular TV star had its disadvantages, one being a lack of privacy. That's why it was so important that she resist the temptation to get to know her new neighbor.

"Sometimes change can be a little sad," Alexis noted.

He sighed. "My dad says change is good. That's why he sold the house. Besides, it didn't feel like our house anymore, not without Mom."

Alexis was about to ask what had happened to his mom when Bryan again looked inside her place and said, "Your apartment's different than ours."

"Would you like to come in?" Alexis found herself inquiring, ignoring the little voice of logic that told her she should send him home.

Eagerly Bryan nodded and followed her in. He pointed out the differences in the location of the fireplace and the color of the carpet.

Since landing her current television role, Alexis had discovered that slipping into her Katie Roberts persona sometimes had its advantages. Katie was always organized and knew her own mind. It was scripted, of course, but that didn't seem to matter. What Alexis couldn't handle, Katie could. With Bryan underfoot and the movers eyeing her expectantly, Alexis knew Katie would come in handy.

"I'm sorry, Bryan, but you're going to have to excuse me," she finally said as he followed her every footstep.

"Are you leaving already?" he asked, matching her steps as she headed for the parking lot.

"No, but I have to get some things from my car."

"I can help!"

Alexis hesitated before saying, "Okay. We'd better hurry, though, because Iggy doesn't like to be kept waiting."

"Iggy?"

Alexis smiled at him. "Just wait and see."

Iggy, as it turned out, was a baby iguana, green with a black banded tail and a comblike crest of scales marching down the center of his back.

"That's *your* lizard?" Bryan asked in amazement. "That's a *girl's* lizard?"

"It's like I tell my sons on 'Two Plus Two.' Girls can be and do and enjoy anything that boys do." She picked up the iguana, and its tail flicked around her arm. "He was a gift from my TV sons, and he really is a unique pet."

Bryan gazed at Alexis with a look of pure devotion. "Can I pet him?"

"You can hold him." She handed him the lizard. "And then you can help me get him settled in his new home."

At the sound of a horn, Alexis turned to see a sleek silver Jaguar pull in next to her. Out stepped a dark-haired man wearing a three-piece suit.

"Ray, I didn't expect to see you." She greeted her publicist with a hug.

"I've come to help you get settled in." He glanced at Bryan inquisitively. "Who's your friend with Iggy?" he asked in a voice only Alexis could hear.

"Ray, this is Bryan Shepard. He lives across the hall from me." Alexis introduced the two, not missing the wariness in Bryan's eyes as he sized up the publicist.

"What happened to your policy not to fraternize with the neighbors?" Again Ray spoke so only she could hear.

"Bryan's going to help me with Iggy," she answered, ignoring his question.

Ray's response was a lift of one brow.

"Come on up and I'll show you the place." She reached for a glass terrarium and handed it to Ray. "You can carry this."

"Better the glass than the iguana," Ray mumbled.

Alexis allowed Bryan to carry Iggy into the apartment building. Then she showed him how to set up Iggy's home—filling the aquarium with rocks, plants and a tiny brass waterfall. By the time they were done, little Iggy had his own miniature jungle right there in the living room, next to the video center.

Alexis asked, "Would anyone like a soft drink?"

"Sure," Bryan answered eagerly.

"I'll take something a little stronger, if you have it," Ray told her, not missing the way Bryan's eyes followed his client's every move.

Alexis fixed Ray a gin and tonic and opened a bottle of mineral water for herself. Then she set a soda in front of Bryan and dropped in a colorful straw.

He gazed at her admiringly. "Mrs. Wahlstrom never uses straws. She says they're a waste of money, but I like them."

"Who's Mrs. Wahlstrom?" Alexis asked.

"My sitter." Bryan's eyes widened. "What time is it?"

Alexis glanced at the Rolex on her wrist. "Five-thirty."

"Uh-oh." Bryan gulped the soda. "I'd better go. Thanks for everything."

"Suppertime, huh?" Alexis said with an understanding smile. "Well, thank you for helping with Iggy."

Bryan was out the door in a flash. As soon as he had gone, Ray commented, "What's with the kid? It's not like you to encourage fans."

"I didn't. I was being neighborly."

Ray chuckled. "Which isn't like you, either." He took a sip of his gin and tonic, then sat pensively.

She sighed. "You're right. I was wrong to invite him in. I don't know why I did it, but he seemed so lonely. The worst part is now I'm going to have to discourage him, and his feelings will be hurt."

"He's just one of millions of kids out there who see Katie Roberts on TV and wish they could have her for a mom," Ray pointed out.

"Yes, well, this particular kid doesn't have a mom." She threw up her hands in frustration. "See? That's another mistake I made. I know too much about him already. I should have handed him an autographed picture the minute he recognized me and sent him home."

"Thank goodness you didn't."

Alexis shot him a wary glance. "What are you talking about?"

He sat forward. "This kid could be just what you need."

Puzzled, she replied, "You're the one who told me to keep my distance from the public."

"That was after the tabloids had a field day with you 'abandoning' your 'starving' siblings."

"I didn't abandon them, and they're not starving. I've been supporting them since I was seventeen, and I still do," she said hotly. It infuriated her that the tabloids could print totally false stories, especially when they concerned her personal life.

"Yes, you and I know that. But once those sleazy papers get hold of something they think will hurt your image, they use it relentlessly. What we need to do is show the media that you are just as maternal as Katie Roberts. What better way than to be a substitute mom to this cute little kid?"

Alexis held up her hand. "Wait a minute. You're not saying I should use this little boy across the hall as a publicity gimmick?" she asked, appalled by the thought.

"What's wrong with having a relationship with a nice, young, motherless boy who could use a maternal influence in his life?" Ray asked innocently.

"No, I won't do it." She folded her arms across her chest.

"Alexis, will you at least think about it?"

"No."

"I'm not asking you to pretend to be nice to the kid. You've already done that without any help from me. Admit it. You liked the kid, didn't you?"

"Yes, but…"

"Then all you have to do is be yourself. Invite him over to play with Iggy, take him out for ice cream, go watch him play ball."

"And you'll conveniently arrange for a photographer to be there, right?"

He shrugged. "What's the difference? They follow you nearly every place you go anyway, don't they?"

"That's not the point. I don't want to involve anyone else in my media circus," she said strongly. "So if you want to remain my publicist, you won't ask me to do such a thing again, got it?"

He held up both hands. "All right, all right."

"Good. Because as far as I'm concerned, Bryan Shepard is a neighbor, and that's all."

Brian opened the door and called out. No one answered.

"Mrs. Wahlstrom? Are you here?" Funny, Mrs. Wahlstrom always told him when she was leaving the apartment. "Is anybody here?"

When there was no answer, Bryan shrugged and moved into the kitchen where he fixed himself a peanut butter and jelly sandwich. He was ensconced in front of the television when his father burst through the door.

"Hi, Dad, I—"

"Where have you been?" Judd roared. His face was flushed, and he looked huge.

"I just made a sandwich—"

"You've been gone three hours. Mrs. Wahlstrom was nearly out of her mind when I got here. She'd been walking all over outside, calling for you. The poor woman has been crying for nearly an hour. She's downstairs right now talking to the police."

The peanut butter stuck in Bryan's throat. The whole time he had been with Katie, Mrs. Wahlstrom had never even entered his mind.

"You stay right here, young man. Don't move. I'll send the police away." Judd turned on his heel and disappeared.

By the time he returned, Bryan had scraped his sandwich into the garbage disposal and turned off the television. He was in big trouble.

Judd sat across from him and leveled an appraising stare that made Bryan feel like a bug pinned to a board. "Well?"

"I just forgot, Dad. Mrs. Wahlstrom told me I could go watch the movers. That's all I was doing, but when Katie asked me to help her with Iggy, I—"

"Who are Katie and Iggy?"

"Katie Roberts from 'Two Plus Two' and her iguana."

Judd rubbed his forehead with his thumb and forefinger. His son's infatuation with the television star had truly gotten out of hand. He was inventing stories about the woman. "Bryan, you know how important it is to tell me the truth."

"I am telling the truth, Dad. Katie Roberts is our new neighbor. You can ask Lenny."

Judd frowned. "You'd better start at the beginning, son."

When the whole story had poured out of Bryan and

he sat silent and spent, Judd spoke.

"So this woman asked you into her apartment and kept you there for three hours without even thinking that someone might be looking for you?"

"Not 'this woman,' Dad. Katie Roberts! And it was my fault, too. After I saw Iggy, I didn't even think about Mrs. Wahlstrom."

Judd restrained a smile, thinking that he, too, might consider an iguana slightly more interesting than the fussy Mrs. W. But his look said none of that.

"Are you sure you're telling me the truth?" Judd drilled his son with a penetrating gaze that would have intimidated the boldest of young men.

"I am, Dad. I swear." He held up his hand, oath style.

Judd had a hard time believing the television star had moved into his building, yet he could always tell when Bryan wasn't being completely honest. This wasn't one of those times.

"You really don't blame Katie Roberts for me being late, do you Dad?"

"You are both at fault. You should never, ever go into a stranger's apartment, nor should you go anywhere without telling your sitter where you'll be. Still, this TV star should have known better than to allow you to stay so long."

"But Katie isn't a stranger. She's on TV every Friday night."

"You may think you know her, Bryan, but you

don't. She must not be a responsible person if she didn't even ask you if your parents knew you were in her apartment."

"She probably forgot because we were having so much fun."

"Mrs. Wahlstrom and I weren't," Judd said flatly, sending the message to Bryan that the conversation was over. "You can spend the evening in your room thinking about what you did and compose a note of apology to Mrs. Wahlstrom while I step across the hall and have a word with our new neighbor."

"No, Dad!" Bryan jumped from his seat. "Don't say anything to her. It was my fault, not hers. Please don't say anything!"

But Judd was already out the door. Perfect TV mom or not, this woman had a few things to learn about children.

CHAPTER TWO

ALEXIS was on a step stool putting dishes away in the tall cupboards when she heard the knock on the door. She was tempted to ignore it.

When the visitor banged for a second time, she climbed from the stool and went to answer the door. Expecting to find the pint-size neighbor boy standing there, she was surprised to see a man. A very handsome man with broad shoulders and thick, muscular arms and a face that looked vaguely familiar to Alexis.

"I'm Bryan Shepard's father."

As soon as he spoke, she made the connection and noticed the similarities. Same thick, dark hair, same chin with the tiny dimple. Same brown eyes that held a hint of sadness.

"I'm Alexis Gordon. Come in." She gestured for him to step inside, automatically flashing a welcoming smile to her new neighbor. He didn't take her offer, but stood with his feet firmly planted in the hallway. She realized it wasn't sadness in his eyes, but annoyance.

"I'd appreciate it if you'd stay away from my son. He's only nine years old and he's not supposed to leave the apartment when I'm not home. You'll just have to find someone else to assist you with your unpacking.''

Alexis was not accustomed to men speaking to her in such a tone. Nor did she appreciate being falsely accused of soliciting help from a child when that child had been the one who had begged to help her. Indignation colored her cheeks and stiffened her spine.

''For your information, Mr. Shepard, I did not drag your son into my apartment to unpack my boxes. He came in to see my pet iguana. I would have sent him home sooner, but he didn't want to leave. He seemed rather lonely, so I let him stay.''

''All afternoon?''

''It was only a couple of hours,'' she protested. She was five feet nine, yet she had to look up at him. She wished he'd come in so she didn't feel as if he was looming in her doorway.

''He's not lonely. He has a sitter, an older woman, and she was worried sick about him because she didn't know where he had gone.''

''If that's the case, I'm sorry, but I hardly think it's my fault. Shouldn't you be scolding your son for not letting her know where he was rather than coming here and making a scene?'' Alexis could feel her cheeks warm as her patience evaporated.

''I already have, but I'm also telling you. You're the adult.''

Alexis took a deep breath. ''Look, all I did was act neighborly. Bryan's a sweet boy.''

The compliment seemed to annoy him further. "The point is, he *is* a boy, and I don't want him leaving the apartment when I'm not home," Judd snapped impatiently.

Alexis was tired of bearing the brunt of this man's anger. "Then you better make sure Bryan understands that," she retorted.

"He does, but he's also an impressionable kid, and you're a TV star."

It was said with such derision it made the hair on the back of Alexis's neck stand on end. "Contrary to what you might want to believe, I haven't eaten any children lately," she said with sugarcoated sarcasm.

"You can save your humor for the TV show. I'm not easily amused." He pierced her with another glare that called attention to his eyes. They weren't just brown, but as rich as the dark chocolate she craved on a regular basis.

She averted her gaze. "Is there anything else, Mr. Shepard? If not, I'm rather busy." Her dismissive tone worked well when she was on the TV set. It didn't work nearly so well with Judd Shepard.

"We'll get along just fine as neighbors as long as you don't encourage Bryan to be anything other than the little boy who lives across the hall. He doesn't need to join the Katie Roberts fan club."

The longer she talked to him, the more obvious his distaste for the television business became. "Maybe you haven't seen the name on the mailbox. It's Alexis

Gordon, not Katie Roberts. Are you sure you're not the one who's confused about that?''

She could see she had hit a nerve. ''I'm not some kid with stars in his eyes, Ms. Gordon. I don't want Bryan over here, and that's that. Understand?''

A chill traveled through her body. She quickly dismissed the disturbing feeling. ''You've made your point, Mr. Shepard. Now I'll make mine. As long as you do your job as a parent, you won't need to be wondering where your son is.'' She folded her arms across her chest and lifted her chin.

He didn't say another word, but turned and walked to the door across the hall. Alexis wondered what kind of woman had been married to him. Bryan had said his mother was gone. Now that she had met the father, it came as no surprise to Alexis. Mr. Shepard was obviously a difficult man.

She closed her door and returned to her boxes in the kitchen. What did it matter? The Shepard boys were nothing to her. She wouldn't see much of them with the long hours she put in on the show. She climbed on the step stool and shoved a large glass dish to the back of the cupboard.

''You don't have to worry, Mr. Shepard,'' she murmured. ''Your little boy's heart is safe.''

Suddenly it dawned on her why he looked so familiar. The day she had made a personal appearance at the mall, he had been the dad who hadn't wanted an autographed picture.

*   *   *

"I don't believe she really lives here."

"She does."

"Then how come I haven't seen her? I've been here four times since you said she moved in and I haven't seen her yet."

"She's here. You can ask my dad, if he ever gets off the phone." For once Bryan's dad was home on a Saturday, but it wasn't much different than when he was at work because he hadn't come out of his office all morning. That's why Bryan had invited Andy Kane over to play. Plus, he wanted to prove to his friend that Katie Roberts lived in his building.

Andy was eleven and thought he was a lot smarter than Bryan. He accused the younger boy of making up the story about Katie Roberts being right across the hall. Unfortunately, since the day she had moved in two weeks ago, Bryan had only seen his new neighbor once, and that was as she drove out of the garage. Today, as usual, Katie Roberts, the perfect mom, was no where in sight. He and Andy had circled the apartment complex at least three times on their bikes, walked through the pool area a dozen times and sat on the steps waiting for a glimpse of her. Bryan knew she was at home, for her red Mercedes sports car was in the garage.

"Why don't we just ring her doorbell?" Andy asked.

"Because I promised my dad I wouldn't do that."

"You don't have to do it. I will." The chubby-faced Andy grinned slyly.

It was tempting, but Bryan thought better of it. Spring break was coming soon, and he didn't need to be grounded for his entire vacation. He turned his attention to the window. Walking along the deck of the pool was a tall, slender blonde wearing a bright orange two-piece suit. Bryan tugged on Andy's shirt sleeve.

"I think that's her! Look!"

Andy pressed his face close to the glass. "It could be, but we need to get closer to see her. Let's go down to the pool!"

The boys sped to the door, only to be stopped by Judd's imposing figure. "Slow down, you two. Where are you going in such a hurry?"

"Outside," Bryan answered.

Judd put a hand of each of their shoulders. "I've got a better idea. How about if I take you over to that baseball card show at the stadium? I hear some of the Dodgers are going to be there giving out autographs. What do you think, Andy? Want to come along?"

"Cool!"

"Can we just go outside for a minute, Dad, and check on our bikes?" Bryan asked. "I'm not sure we locked them up."

"I'll tell you what. You grab a snack and I'll run downstairs. I need to get some stuff out of the car, anyway. I'll check on the bikes for you, okay?"

Before the boys could protest, Judd was heading for the door. "Make sure you wait here. I'm expecting an important phone call and I don't want to miss it."

As he disappeared, the boys groaned. Then they raced to the window.

"Now how are we going to see if it's her?"

"It's her. I can tell," Bryan told his friend.

"I can't. You don't know for sure it is."

Bryan's face lit up. "I'll get my dad's binoculars. Wait here."

When he returned he carried a pair of black field glasses. He held them to his eyes, his fingers pushing on the center focus piece. After a few seconds, he handed the glasses to his friend, a triumphant grin on his face. "Look for yourself. It's her."

Andy raised the binoculars to his eyes. "Wow! It *is* her! She's a babe!"

"No, she's not. She's nice."

Andy continued to stare at Alexis through the glasses. "She looks like she's going to go in for a swim."

"Let me look," Bryan begged.

"Wait until I've finished," Andy argued, not wanting to relinquish the field glasses.

They began to play tug-of-war with the binoculars. A large hand intervened.

"Give me the glasses," Judd said firmly.

Looking as guilty as if they'd been caught with their hands in a cookie jar, they released their hold on the binoculars. "We were just looking at the birds and stuff," Bryan began.

"Did you have your snack yet?" Judd asked. When

both boys shook their heads, he pointed them in the direction of the kitchen. "Do it now. As soon I get my phone call, we'll leave."

Judd watched the two boys slink off to the kitchen. *Birds and stuff?* What was so interesting, he wondered, as he panned the recreation area bordered with palm trees and flowering shrubs. Most of the apartment dwellers sunbathed on the lounge chairs.

There was, however, one woman cutting a swath through the pool, her blonde hair plastered against her scalp as she butterflied in and out of the water. Judd raised the binoculars to his eyes. It was his neighbor across the hall.

So *that's* why Bryan and Andy were fighting over the field glasses. They wanted to get a closer look at the TV star.

As she boosted herself out of the pool, Judd felt something tighten in his chest. Wearing nothing but an orange two-piece swim suit, Alexis Gordon was not likely to be mistaken for anyone's mom. Perfectly proportioned with enough curves to catch any man's eye, she looked like a goddess rising out of the water.

As she squeezed the water from her hair, Judd's heartbeat accelerated. She appeared fragile as she stood at the edge of the pool, yet he knew she had to be tough to survive in the entertainment industry.

He appraised her from head to toe and discovered there was not a flaw on her perfectly shaped body. She had great legs, great hands, great feet...great everything. As he watched her pat the water from her flesh with the large beach towel, he wondered about her personal life. He knew she wasn't married, but did she have a boyfriend?

"Dad?"

Judd nearly dropped the field glasses at the sound of Bryan's voice.

"Can me and Andy have a soda?" he asked innocently.

"Ah, sure. Go ahead." Judd fidgeted with the strap on the binoculars, feeling as guilty as Bryan had looked only a short time before. He lifted the field glasses. "I'm just going to put these away and we'll go, okay?"

"Okay." Judd wondered if his son had seen him ogling Alexis Gordon. For that's exactly what he had been doing. And enjoying every minute of it.

As Alexis walked to the parking garage, she heard two young voices. It didn't take her long to realize that one of them belonged to the boy across the hall.

"This game is dumb and boring."

"I know, but Dad said we couldn't throw darts any more. He had to pay to have the wall fixed."

"There must be something better to do. Maybe we could pitch these."

"I don't know. Dad said—"

"We can't throw *darts*. But these aren't darts."

Alexis had no idea what the boys were talking about. However, she soon found out. When she backed her gleaming red Mercedes out of her parking stall, a rock ricocheted off the front bumper with a sharp ping.

She slammed on the brakes and jumped out of the car. She was already massaging the glaring chip in the finish when the boys reached her.

"We're sorry. We didn't even hear you start your car. Andy didn't see you back out until it was too late," Bryan spoke in a rush, nearly in tears.

"Look what you've done to my brand-new car!"

"It was an accident," Bryan pleaded through the sobs welling in his throat.

Alexis counted to ten. Once, twice and then a third time before she had her emotions in check. For the past week she had managed to avoid her obnoxious neighbor's child. Now this.

The older boy's face was red, but Bryan looked as if he might burst into tears any moment. Even in her anger, Alexis could see he was steeped in remorse. Still, she couldn't let her sympathy get in the way.

"Maybe I should have a talk with both of your fathers about this."

"No!" the older boy wailed.

Judd appeared with a stack of cardboard boxes destined for the recycling bin. "What's going on here?" He pinned Alexis with a steely gaze. "What have you done to these boys?"

"Me? Done something to them? The question is, what have they done to my car?"

Judd turned to the Mercedes and saw the scratched paint. "The boys did that?"

"Yes. Playing their little game."

He took a foam ball from his son's hand. "This couldn't have chipped your paint. You must have got that little beauty mark somewhere else."

Alexis hated his smugness. She gestured to the ball. "They weren't throwing that. They were throwing rocks from the garden."

"Rocks?" Judd's tone was annoyingly dubious. "Bryan knows better than to do something like that."

Alexis felt her impatience growing with this big dense hunk of a man. How could anyone so gorgeous be so blind to the foibles of his son? "I was in my car, I pulled out of my spot and bingo, a rock hit my fender."

"Did you honk and let them know you were coming?" he asked.

"You think it's *my* fault?" Alexis stared at him in disbelief. "Your child was playing a dangerous game. And I shouldn't have to point out that this is a parking lot, not a playground. What kind of a parent are you, anyway?" she continued. "Boys shouldn't have to entertain themselves throwing rocks!"

"If they *were* throwing rocks."

"They were," Alexis said firmly.

Judd turned to his son. "Were you throwing rocks?"

Bryan's answer was to burst into tears.

Judd's face darkened. "How could you do such a thing?"

"I'm sorry, Dad," the little boy apologized through a mask of grief.

"Don't tell *me* you're sorry. Tell *her*," Judd ordered him.

"I did," he sobbed. "But she's really mad at me."

Alexis felt swamped with emotion. Suddenly, her car didn't seem important. What mattered was this little boy, who was crying his heart out because she was angry at him. It struck her that Bryan had cried a lot in his young life, tears of grief far deeper than these.

"We'll pay for the damages," Judd said in as close to an apology as Alexis thought he was going to make.

"Who's we? You or Bryan?"

His lip curled disdainfully. "You think I should pay?"

"You're the parent," she told him, then slid her long, graceful body into the car. "I would think, being a father, you would know boys need supervision and direction. It's only natural they're going to get into trouble if they're left alone."

"And where do those words of wisdom come from? The TV studio? Or did you learn them in an acting class?"

She would have liked to wipe the smug expression off his face. "I'm not the one pretending to be the parent here," she said sweetly, then revved the engine and pulled away.

Judd, Bryan and Andy were left standing, staring after her.

"She was awesome," Bryan murmured, his tears stopped. "She sounded just like she does on television."

"Yeah," Andy concurred. "All that stuff about boys needing supervision and direction. Cool."

Judd felt as if he'd been hit in the face with a rock. She'd fussed and fumed, and the boys thought she was awesome? He wondered what they were going to think of him when he grounded them both for their deed.

Judd worked the following Saturday. He hated the fact that he often had to choose between helping people or spending time with his son. On this occasion, had he not chosen work, a life would have been lost.

He unlocked his mailbox and pulled out the stack of envelopes. Striding down the hallway, he thumbed through a collection of bills and junk mail. When he came to a pink envelope, he sighed. It was addressed to Alexis Gordon.

Judd couldn't hand it to the building supervisor, because his office closed at noon on Saturdays. If he waited until Monday morning, the letter wouldn't be delivered for two days. On the chance that the letter was important, he decided to do the neighborly thing. He knocked on Alexis Gordon's door.

To his surprise, she didn't open it. Instead, she called out, "It's open. Come on in."

Judd thought it rather strange that she would invite someone in without asking who it was. Even though it was a building with a good security system, it was risky leaving a door unlocked in any apartment complex.

When he stepped inside, he saw why Alexis Gordon hadn't answered personally. She was on her hands and knees in the kitchen, a wide paintbrush in hand, a bucket of white paste beside her. A long strip of wallpaper stretched from one end of the floor to the other. She looked very different from the actress who had signed autographs at the mall. Her face was scrubbed free of makeup and her hair was pulled back in a ponytail. There were no rings on her fingers, no gold chains around her neck, no red polish on her fingernails, no high heels on her feet. She could have been any ordinary woman next door, only she wasn't ordinary. Far from it. She was lovely, even when she was up to her elbows in paste.

"Oh! I thought you were Jenny, our neighbor down the hall. She's helping me with this." Alexis continued to brush paste on the back of the wallpaper.

"You shouldn't leave your door unlocked," Judd told her, trying not to notice the gentle swell of flesh that wanted to pop right out of the scoop neck of her shirt.

"This building has tight security," she pointed out, not looking at him. She brought the ends of the wallpaper to the center, then folded it in two. "Besides, Jenny said she'd be right back, and I didn't want her to be locked out." Finally, she looked at him. "What can I do for you, Judd?"

"I brought you this." He held up the pink envelope. "It was in my mailbox by mistake."

She didn't bother looking at it, but said, "Would you mind putting it on the table? My hands have paste on them."

So did her denim shorts, which revealed smooth, creamy white legs. Judd quickly pulled his eyes away and did as she asked. Then he glanced at the kitchen wall and saw that a flower border extended halfway around it. "Is that the other half?"

She nodded. "I wonder what happened to Jenny? I've already pasted this piece, and if I don't put it up soon..." She trailed off, a look of appeal in her green eyes.

Judd saw a small stepladder at one end of the kitchen and a wooden chair at the opposite end. From the look in her eye, he knew she wanted him to help her.

"I have no experience with wallpaper," he told her before she could ask the question.

She flapped her hand in the air. "Oh, don't worry. There's nothing to it. I just need you to hold one end so I can get the other end started." She didn't wait for his consent, but carefully unfolded the strip of wallpaper, saying, "I'll stand on the chair and you can have the ladder. Just line up your end with that pencil mark on the wall." She hopped onto the wooden chair. It annoyed him that she assumed he would come to her rescue. "I can't help you."

"Can't or won't?" she challenged him from her lofty perch.

There was something in the pose she struck that compelled him to set his stack of mail on the counter. He reached for the other end of the wallpaper border and climbed the stepladder.

"Down a bit. Now up. Watch the middle," she directed, smoothing the paper in place. By the time she had finished, his fingers were covered with paste.

"You can rinse your hands off in the sink," she told him, continuing to smooth the border with a bristly brush. When she was satisfied with her efforts, she stood back and admired her work. "There. I think I like it."

Judd dried his hands on a paper towel. "How come you didn't hire someone to do this?" he asked.

"Because I like to hang wallpaper," she answered. "It's fun."

He cast her a dubious glance. "Did you get your car fixed?"

"Yes, and the good news is because I needed a couple of other spots touched up, they didn't charge me for the mark left by the rock."

"Bryan can pay you something anyway. He's giving up his allowance for a month," said Judd.

"Why? It isn't costing you anything," she pointed out.

"He still needs to be punished. He and Andy can't

play together for a week, either. Both those little guys need to learn to put their brains in gear before they act.''

''Isn't that a little harsh?''

Judd retrieved his mail from the counter. ''Maybe, but he disobeyed and did something that could have caused serious injury—if not to your car, to a human being.''

He wished she would let the matter drop, but she continued to champion his son. ''But the point is, he didn't hurt anybody. And it wasn't even Bryan who threw the rock. It was his friend.''

''So you think I should let the entire incident go by without punishing him?''

''He's already been grounded. Is it necessary for him to lose his allowance, too?''

Judd's brow furrowed. ''You've been talking to Bryan again, haven't you?''

She straightened her spine and crossed her arms. ''I did accidentally run into him in the hallway. I invited him in, but he was an obedient child and went home, instead.''

''I thought we had agreed you wouldn't encourage him to visit.''

''He wanted to see Iggy.''

''The iguana.'' Judd looked around warily. Did she let the lizard run free in the apartment? ''I'll speak to him about that. He shouldn't be bothering you.''

''He's not bothering me. Young boys like pets,'' she told him.

"And you would know what young boys like since you're a TV mom, is that it? Just like being a TV mom makes you an expert on discipline?"

Alexis had worked with plenty of difficult men and had become adept at dealing with them. Determined not to let him rattle her, she said evenly, "Look, I'm not Katie Roberts at the moment. I'm Alexis Gordon, single woman, no children. But that doesn't mean I didn't notice the way Bryan handled Iggy. He liked playing with him. Which is something you might want to keep in mind. He could use a pet."

Judd nearly choked. As if he'd allow a slimy lizard in his apartment. Again his eyes did a quick survey of the room, looking for the iguana, expecting it to leap out from behind the sofa or from atop the drapes.

"I don't think Mrs. Wahlstrom could handle an iguana," he told her.

"They're quite simple, actually, though they do grow to be quite large. No, I was thinking more along the lines of a cat or a dog."

Jenny waltzed in the door. "Hi. Sorry I'm late, but I got a phone call I had to take." When she saw Judd, her eyes widened with interest. "I don't think we've met. I'm Jenny Lee Williams." She glanced curiously from Judd to Alexis.

"This is Judd Shepard. He lives across the hall," Alexis told her.

"I'm surprised we haven't met before." Jenny smiled as they shook hands.

"He works odd hours," Alexis answered for Judd, who wondered how she knew.

Of course, the answer was Bryan. His son must have had quite a talk with the actress, which only added to Judd's annoyance. It made him wonder what else Bryan had told his neighbor.

"I'd better get home. The sitter's with Bryan," Judd said, then excused himself with a polite goodbye.

As he left, Alexis called out, "Thanks for the help with the wallpaper. And if you need help picking out that iguana…"

As he walked out the door, she chuckled, and Judd couldn't resist one last look at Alexis Gordon, the paperhanger. She grinned. To his irritation, he had to fight the urge to grin right back.

CHAPTER THREE

IT WAS almost nine when Alexis got home from the studio on Monday. Her first stop was the Shepard apartment. In her pocket she had two tickets for the Thursday taping of "Two Plus Two." Because Judd had helped her with the wallpaper, she thought it would be nice to say thank-you, especially since Bryan was a fan of the show.

Expecting Judd to answer the door, Alexis was surprised when Bryan was the one who undid the chain lock and motioned for her to come inside. He was barefoot and in his pajamas, looking sleepy. When he realized who it was, he perked right up.

"Katie! Hi!"

"I'm sorry, Bryan. Did I get you out of bed?" She apologized, glancing around the apartment for his father.

"It's all right. I'm usually awake until Dad gets home." He grabbed her by the hand and pulled her inside. "This is really cool—you coming to see me."

"Your father's not here?"

"Uh-uh. He's working."

"And you're home alone? Where's Mrs. Wahlstrom?"

"She fell asleep on the couch." Bryan nodded toward the living room, where the older woman lay stretched out on the sofa. "I'm really glad you came over. Do you want to see my room?"

"It's awfully late. Maybe I'll have a look another time, okay?" She softened her refusal with a tender smile. "I came over because I have something for you." She reached into her pocket and pulled out the tickets. "These are for the taping of 'Two Plus Two.'"

Bryan's eyes lit up. "Cool! Thanks, Katie!"

It was the second time he had called her by her stage name. "Why don't you call me Alexis, Bryan? I'm not on television right now."

"But you seem like Katie to me," he said with a shy grin that was so endearing, she found it difficult to be upset with him. He stared at the tickets in his hands.

"There's a ticket for you and one for your dad for Thursday afternoon."

His little face fell. "My dad has to be at work on Thursdays, all day."

"I bet he can take some time off," she said optimistically.

His face remained sober. "Uh-uh. His job's real important."

But surely not more important than his child, Alexis reasoned. If it were, Judd Shepard had his values all mixed up. So far her impression of the man was not a favorable one. He left his son alone far too often.

Obviously he was a workaholic. Her heart ached for the small boy who looked so sad.

"I'll tell you what. I'll leave a note for your father, and we'll see what we can do to make this happen for you, okay?" She flashed him a smile of encouragement. He nodded eagerly.

She was enjoying the feel of the sun on her body as she lay by the pool after her morning swim when Judd finally caught up with her. The muscles in her stomach tensed. From his expression, she could see that he was not happy. Just what she didn't need—a confrontation with Bryan's dad. There had been a lot of tension on the set all week because of camera problems. She didn't need additional stress.

Judd had worked all night. The last thing he wanted was to have words with an actress who had nothing better to do than sun herself and hand out studio tickets to his son. He worked in a life-and-death business while this woman played make-believe for a living.

He was going to make this encounter brief and to the point. No tickets, no thanks. That was it.

When she ran a finger under the top of her very sparse two-piece bathing suit, Judd's motive for speaking to her grew hazy. The tiny scraps of orange fabric emphasized every delectable curve on her body.

He looked away, reminding himself that he'd come to return the tickets. There was no way he could bring Bryan to the taping. What's more, the boy's imagination was already too active, as far as Judd was concerned. Bryan assumed television life was reality. That was apparent by the way he called their neighbor Katie, even though Katie Roberts didn't exist outside the television set!

But Alexis Gordon definitely *did* exist. In glorious, full-bodied, voluptuous color. That was obvious as she lay sunning on a lounge chair, her skin oiled and glistening. Judd felt his mouth go dry. She was a beautiful woman, he'd have to give her that.

Then she shifted and did this little thing with her finger and the skimpy top of her suit, and Judd thought he was going to have to sit down. Fantasies filled his head. Of what it would be like to swim with her, to apply oil to her skin, to lay close to her. He shook his head and reminded himself why he was there.

"Ms. Gordon?"

"Hi, neighbor." Her voice was husky and inviting. "Looking for Bryan?"

"No. Actually, I'm looking for you."

She swung her feet off the chaise and sat forward. "I'm right here, Judd."

She was a smooth one, Judd thought, noting the flirtatious pose and the way she said his name—as if he had come for other reasons, none of them concerning a child. "I wanted to return these." He pulled the tickets from his pocket and watched her face fall.

"You aren't going to bring Bryan to the taping?"

"It's not possible."

"But those tickets are a thank-you from me—for

helping with my wallpaper.'' She batted her long lashes at him with an innocence he guessed came from years of practice.

''You don't need to give me anything for helping you.''

''But I wanted to do this for you and Bryan.''

The sincerity in her eyes made him soften his words. ''It was a nice gesture, but I can't get away from work.''

''Oh.'' She made a sound of disappointment. ''What about Mrs. Wahlstrom? Couldn't she bring him?''

''That's not going to work out, either.''

The sun slipped behind a cloud, and she reached for a white cotton shirt. She slipped it over her shoulders but left it unbuttoned, allowing Judd a tantalizing view of her bosom.

''Maybe he has an aunt or an uncle who could bring him?'' she suggested.

''No, he doesn't.''

She folded her arms. ''You don't want him there, do you?''

He shook his head. ''I don't think it's a good idea.''

''I don't see why not. Bryan would absolutely love it. I could take him on a tour of the studio. And I know he'd enjoy meeting the boys who play my sons.''

''That's exactly why I don't feel comfortable bringing him. Bryan is obsessed with that television program already. The last thing he needs is an overdose of fantasy.''

''Oh, is that so?'' Alexis challenged him, rising to her feet. ''It seems to me that Bryan *needs* a little fantasy in his life. He's certainly experienced enough reality!''

''What is that supposed to mean?''

''You're rarely there for the little boy. He spends most of his time with an elderly woman, waiting for you to return.''

''I have a job that requires long hours. I can hardly drop by the apartment during work.'' Judd didn't want to be sarcastic, yet it came naturally at the sight of soft skin bulging from the top of her swimsuit.

''Bryan understands what an important job you do, but you have to understand that he's a child. He doesn't talk as if he has much fun in his life.''

''Well, sometimes life isn't fun, is it?'' he asked bitterly, thinking of the past year's loneliness. ''It's not as rosy as your TV program would like us all to believe.''

''Maybe that's why you should bring him to a taping. You say you're worried about him confusing fantasy with reality. Well, this is a good way to show him the difference. When he sees how the program is made, with the sets and the cameras and the cue cards, he'll have a better understanding of how it's created. He'll see that it really is make-believe.''

As much as Judd hated to admit it, she made sense.

He rubbed the back of his neck. "I'll have to see if I can get someone to cover for me at work."

"Does that mean you'll do it if you can get away from your job?"

"Just this once. But don't give us tickets again. As far as I'm concerned, you're only encouraging him to continue to see you as the perfect mom, when really you're just a...starlet."

"Is that supposed to be a slam at me?"

She was laughing at him! Judd knew he had to leave or risk saying—or doing—something he'd regret. "You can take it any way you wish, Ms. Gordon." Dragging his eyes from her, he turned and left.

Alexis didn't see either of the Shepards again until early Wednesday morning. It was still dark when she dragged herself out of bed, pulled on a pair of shorts and a T-shirt, then headed for the parking garage. As she unlocked the door of her convertible, Judd's Jeep Cherokee pulled into the stall beside her.

Alexis could see he was tired by the way he slowly climbed out of the vehicle. One look at his face told her he had been up all night.

"You're just getting home from work now?"

He paused beside his car and looked at her. "Look, I've had a really bad night. I don't need you to lecture me about leaving my son home with a baby-sitter."

She breathed a sigh of relief. "So there was someone with him."

He nodded. "Mrs. Wahlstrom. Did you think I'd leave him home alone?"

"No," she said quickly, although the thought had crossed her mind.

"Despite what you think, I'm not a bad parent," he said firmly.

"I never said you were." She felt a rush of sympathy for him. The man was exhausted. It couldn't be easy being a single father. "I was just concerned for Bryan, that's all."

"Well, that makes two of us," he said wearily.

There was a vulnerability in him she hadn't seen before. Alexis wished she could erase those dark lines shadowing his handsome face. She wondered what it would be like to smooth away the fatigue and stress from his cheeks and jaw. How would his skin feel beneath her fingers? Was it as rough as it looked? Realizing the direction her thoughts were taking, she decided it was time to end the conversation. "Well, I have to go. I'm on my way to the studio." She climbed into the Mercedes and turned the key. Only nothing happened.

Over and over she tried to start the car, with no luck. Judd pulled her door open and said, "Sounds like you're not going anywhere."

She glanced at her watch. "Just great. I'm already running behind." She reached for her cellular phone.

"What are you doing?"

"Calling a tow."

"That's not necessary. I can take a look at it for you."

She stopped dialing to look at him. Good Samaritan was not a role she would have expected him to play—at least not with her. "You'd do that for me?"

He nodded. "Pop the hood."

Alexis did as instructed, then watched as he bent over and peered at the engine. While his fingers wiggled and poked at various wires and bolts, she studied his face, fascinated by the way it changed as he went from confused to triumphant. When he looked up and caught her staring, she blushed like a schoolgirl.

"Loose battery cable," he muttered.

She nodded, then quickly looked away.

"That will get you to where you're going, but you should probably stop at a service station and have it checked by a mechanic," he told her.

Alexis could see the weariness in his face. She fought the urge to smooth the hair from his brow and tell him to get some sleep. Instead she said, "Thanks. I appreciate your help."

He gave her a ghost of a smile and said, "You're welcome." Then he slowly ambled away.

Alexis backed out of the parking place. No matter how hard she tried, she couldn't resist looking in her rearview mirror. She wanted to get one last look at Judd, to feel that little tingle of pleasure she was coming to expect whenever she saw him.

*   *   *

Alexis found Bryan Shepard sitting outside her door when she arrived home from the studio that evening.

"Do you think I could come in and play with Iggy?"

The last thing she wanted was company. Her head ached and she was tired, yet there was something about this little boy that made her say yes.

"Sure. Go tell your baby-sitter where you are."

"I don't have a baby-sitter today. My dad's home."

Alexis wondered if it was because Judd had worked straight through the night. "You need to tell your dad where you're going to be," she reminded him.

Bryan was off like a shot. Alexis expected he wouldn't return, that Judd would forbid his son to visit her, but to her surprise, Bryan was back at her door in no time. She let him in, and he went straight to the terrarium, where Iggy gave him a slow blink.

"He knows me!" Bryan shouted with glee as he picked up the little lizard. He stared at Alexis. "I sure am glad you talked my dad into taking me to the taping of your show tomorrow."

"I think both of you will enjoy it," Alexis said, suppressing a yawn.

"Are you tired? If you want to take a nap, I can leave."

Alexis smiled. "I *am* tired. And you are the first person today who was polite enough to ask about me. Thank you."

"Why are you tired? I'd never be tired if I could work on television." Bryan put Iggy on the carpet.

"Oh, yes, you would. The twins were exhausted today and therefore very naughty."

"Kip and Cody?"

"Yes, only their real names are Martin and MacLean."

"They're so lucky," he said with an envious sigh. "They have two moms."

The look in Bryan's eyes tugged on her heartstrings. "I'm not really their mother, Bryan," Alexis reminded him.

"But you like them, right?"

"Oh, yes. Very much." She smiled at the odd question. "Why do you ask?"

"Because when I watch the show you look like you really love them. Like you really are their mom." His voice grew wistful. "Like my mom used to look at me."

"Where is your mom, Bryan?" she asked gently.

"In heaven."

Alexis had to swallow the lump in her throat. "I see."

"She went with Toby," he said quietly.

"Toby?"

"He was our dog. They were out for a walk one day and they got hit by a car."

It was said so matter-of-factly that Alexis might have thought Bryan didn't feel any pain talking about the subject. But then she looked into his eyes, and she saw the grief that wasn't in his voice.

"I'm sorry, Bryan. You must miss her."

He reached for Iggy and rubbed his scaly skin. "She made me chocolate chip pancakes with whipped cream. And she was always home. She'd touch my forehead right before I went to sleep and it felt nice."

Alexis couldn't stand the ache the child's words put in her heart. Her mother had died when she was sixteen, leaving a void in her life that couldn't be filled. When a knock sounded on the door, Alexis knew that Judd Shepard had come looking for his son. "I bet that's your dad."

"He's taking me out for pizza," Bryan explained. "Maybe you want to come?"

The eager brightness in his expression hurt her almost as much as the pain he'd shown when he mentioned his mother. This child was so vulnerable and so personable that he was worming his way past her defenses.

Before she could respond, the door opened and Judd filled the doorway. He was wearing soft, faded jeans and a white short-sleeved shirt open at the collar. His feet were bare inside scuffed creamy leather loafers. He looked so...touchable. The hard edges were gone from his eyes and face. Why did he have to look so darned vulnerable? It was easier to remember he was impossible when he didn't look like...like what?

A movie star? Hardly. Alexis wasn't impressed by

them anymore. She'd just about had it with big egos.
No, tonight he looked like a father. *And,* said the imp
in her mind, *a husband without a wife.*

"I asked her to come with us, Dad," Bryan reported eagerly. "It's okay, isn't it?"

The fleeting look of consternation that crossed
Judd's face told Alexis it was far from okay, but his
words were measured and polite. "Of course. We're
going to the place just down the block. They do a
very good deep-dish supreme."

Alexis found it difficult to say no, but she knew
Judd didn't want her to come along. "I'm sorry, but
I'm really tired tonight. But thanks for asking."

Bryan groaned, which caused Judd's mouth to
tighten.

"Do you think the next time we go get pizza Katie
can come with us?" Bryan pleaded, his voice thick
with disappointment.

Judd's eyes narrowed and Alexis expected he'd say
no. To her surprise, however, he said, "We'll see. I'm
sure *Alexis* has a busy schedule."

Bryan got the message. "Oops, I'm mean Alexis.
Sorry," he apologized with a sweet smile that made
her want to give him a quick hug. But with Judd
standing there, she thought it would be better not to.

Judd seemed no more in a hurry to leave than
Bryan. They stood in the doorway shifting from foot
to foot like a pair of uncertain teenage swains.

"I was going to get out some fresh fruit and veg-
gies for supper," Alexis finally said. "You could

have an appetizer with me before you go get your pizza.''

"Awright!'' Bryan bolted into the room as if jet-propelled. "Have you got toothpicks and dip? That's the way my mom used to serve it.''

Pain spread over Judd's face. Alexis turned away. He was still in love with his dead wife, that was for sure. Another reason not to think of him as anything but a neighbor. She needed a man with an eye on the future.

They made a party of the snacks, rounding them out with wine for the adults and grape juice for Bryan. As they munched on carrot and celery sticks, Alexis wondered what Judd was thinking. His face revealed little as he listened to Bryan chat about the upcoming visit to the studio.

When Alexis stood to replenish the vegetables, Judd stopped her. "We've had plenty, thanks. Right, Bryan?'' He ruffled his son's hair. "We'd better go get that pizza.''

"Can we get the extra large?'' Bryan jumped to his feet.

"I think I may have to take on an extra job just to keep you in groceries,'' Judd said with a laugh.

Bryan's goodbye was lovely and natural, Judd's less so.

"I'll see you tomorrow at the taping,'' she called to the retreating figures.

As she closed the door, Alexis felt a twinge of regret. It might have been fun to go out for pizza with

the Shepard boys. Then she mentally scolded herself.
She would have to be careful not to get attached to
either of them. At the end of this season, she had
plans.

Her agent said a feature film was in the offing. That
was sounding better and better all the time. A weekly
sitcom was grueling. Long hours, little free time. For
the past three years she had worked hard to save
enough money so she could say goodbye to
Hollywood. She wanted to go home to Colorado, to
her family—the real one, her two sisters and her
brother. She could shoot movies on location and return to the place where she felt more centered, more
real. It would be the best of both worlds.

Alexis had definite plans for the future. This was
not the time to be starting a relationship—especially
with a young boy who needed a mother. Or his father,
who didn't appear to need anyone.

What she needed to do was focus on the future. A
future that didn't include the Shepard boys. No matter
how cute they were.

CHAPTER FOUR

FRIDAY morning, Judd was whistling as he entered the air terminal that housed Lifeline Flying Service. A night's uninterrupted sleep and breakfast with Bryan had worked wonders. He hadn't realized how much pressure he'd been feeling as the demand for his air ambulance service had increased.

It had taken its toll on both him and Bryan. A boy needed his father—particularly Bryan and especially right now. Proof of that was his son's infatuation with the beautiful Alexis from across the hall. If Judd hadn't been forced to spend so much time away from home, Bryan wouldn't be following the television star around as if he were a lost puppy in search of a home.

That was going to change. What Bryan needed was a good role model and a little father-son time. With patience and understanding, Judd would see to it that Bryan's crush on the alluring Alexis was short-lived. They'd gone to the taping, done the studio tour and said goodbye. He hoped that would be the end of their socializing.

Feeling good and exceptionally confident, Judd sauntered past the receptionist's desk where Frankie Floyd sat reading the latest newspaper tabloid. Her peroxide blond hair was a frizzy halo around her face and emphasized her pale complexion and bright red lipstick.

Judd found it amusing that someone as intelligent as Frankie thought the tabloids were filled with the gospel truth. He knew she practically inhaled every article, from the horoscope chart to the last tidbit of gossip. Thankfully, she was also an efficient secretary with a no-nonsense manner on the telephone. She could dispatch rescue aircraft without hesitation.

"No new emergencies, I'm glad to report," she greeted him. "It was an unusually quiet night."

"Thank goodness." He tapped on her newspaper and asked, "Any aliens been born to movie stars this week? Or women feeling better after having their heads surgically reattached? Oh, and is Elvis still selling cars at that used car dealer on Harrison Avenue?"

"No, no and no." Frankie harrumphed. "You are such a cynic! Lots of the stories in the tabloids are true. Just because they toss in a few weird items for entertainment value doesn't mean every story is false."

Judd poured himself a cup of coffee.

"Here's why I really like to read these things. You can get the latest scoop on who's dating who in Hollywood," Frankie said with excessive delight. "Look. There's Alexis Gordon from 'Two Plus Two.' Talk about a picture saying more than a thousand words!"

The grin disappeared from Judd's face as he leaned

over to take a look. Coffee sloshed out of his cup onto the desk.

The photo was of Alexis, all right, taken as she and a man with dark hair and sleepy, sexy eyes exited a posh Beverly Hills bistro. Alexis wore a pale, strapless evening gown that barely contained her ample bosom. Her hair was a controlled riot of curls that enhanced the perfection of her features. Though she had shied away from the camera, her companion had stared straight into the lens with a wide, almost triumphant smile.

It was no wonder to Judd that the man was grinning. He had his trophy right there on his arm. The thought sent a funny little pain wiggling through Judd's stomach.

"Listen to this," Frankie continued, unaware of Judd's discomfort. "'Sitcom star Alexis Gordon is seen out on the town with unidentified new heartthrob. Now the question is, can one man satisfy a woman this beautiful, successful and talented? Everyone in Hollywood knows she changes beaus like she changes shoes. She's broken many hearts in the past. Is this handsome fellow destined for disappointment as well?'"

Judd thought the man looked like a grown-up version of Bryan, only instead of puppy love in his eyes there was lust. He grimaced at the thought.

"Do you suppose that's really her boyfriend or just some guy she happens to know?" Frankie mused.

"I've never seen him hanging around," Judd muttered.

"What? Why would you see him—or her?" Frankie fixed him with an inquisitive stare.

Judd knew he might as well confess. "Alexis Gordon lives across the hall from me."

Frankie gasped. "You're kidding!" She looked at him as if he had just said the president had dined at his home last night.

"No offense, boss, but I expected her to live in one of those million-dollar mansions. Not that your place isn't great, but she must make tons of money."

He shrugged. "The complex is rather secluded."

"Maybe she's not the showy type." Frankie groaned as she returned her attention to the tabloid. "Although look at that dress! I bet it's a designer original." She sighed. "What I wouldn't give to wear something like that and look that good."

"I like you just the way you are, Frankie. What's important is that you don't pretend to be something you're not. Like the perfect mother," he said with a sneer.

"But that's her job as an actress," Frankie pointed out. "She's paid to be the ideal mother for those two little boys on TV."

"She looks anything but motherly in that photo." Judd realized his finger was shaking as he pointed to the seductive photo. It landed on the voluptuous swell of her breast.

"I bet that despite what this newspaper says, she's

a nice person," Frankie countered. "She couldn't be that likable a TV character if she wasn't a bit like that in real life."

"Now you're starting to sound like my son." Judd couldn't keep the disapproval from his voice. "Must I remind you that she's *acting* when she plays that role? Her world is make-believe."

"Yes, but I don't think she would have taken that part unless she had strong maternal feelings. And I don't think she could put so much emotion into acting if she didn't possess some of it herself."

Judd didn't agree, but he didn't want to argue with his dispatcher. Fortunately the phone rang, putting an end to the discussion. Within seconds, the tabloid paper was cast aside as Frankie took down the emergency information.

His jaw set and his eyes steely, Judd prepared his crew for another medical transport. But no matter how hard Judd tried to forget that picture in the tabloid, he couldn't. Often during the remainder of the day he saw Alexis Gordon in her strapless gown with her bosom threatening to fall out of its bodice. He'd never wanted Bryan to hang around with the TV star in the first place. Now he knew that his friendship with her must end. Alexis was a dual personality. She might hurt and disillusion his son. The last thing his child needed was a make-believe mom—especially one like Alexis.

"Can I, Dad? Huh? Can I? It would be so totally cool! Nobody would be able to tease me any more or call me a liar because I said Katie Roberts lived across the hall from us.''

''Her name is Alexis, not Katie, and no, you can't take her to show-and-tell at school. She's a very busy actress. Kids take favorite toys or projects they've made to show-and-tell, not people.'' Judd found this begging to be getting old. Bryan had been at it all evening. It was not a subject Judd wanted to discuss.

''That's not true,'' Bryan argued. ''Julie McCarty brought her dad to school because he's a postman. He wore his uniform and carried that big sack on his back and answered all kinds of questions about his job. Everybody said that was the best show-and-tell ever— except for the time Owen Cartwright brought his brother's boa constrictor and it got loose in the classroom. That was really cool.''

''Why not bring those agates your grandfather polished up and sent to you?'' Judd suggested.

''No one wants to see some dumb old rocks when they can meet Katie Roberts in person,'' he said with a sigh.

''But that's the point. They can't meet her in person.''

''Why not?''

''Because if I've said it once, I've said it a dozen times. No!'' he bellowed. ''Now go get ready for bed and I'll come say good-night.''

''Aw, Dad.'' Bryan moaned and slunk away, shoulders drooping.

For once Judd didn't feel guilty about denying his son's request. He knew he was doing the right thing. Judd squared his shoulders and went to say goodnight to his son.

He stopped in the doorway. Bryan was on his knees by the bed, intently saying his nightly prayers. Hesitant to interrupt the ritual Bryan's mother had begun, Judd stood listening.

"Dear God, thanks for everything good You gave me today. I can't remember what it all is right now, but I do know that we had a great school lunch. And thanks for watching my mom for me. Tell her hi and that I really miss her."

Judd felt the familiar constriction around his heart. Would the time ever come when they would stop missing Carol?

"Bless Dad and Mrs. Wahlstrom. And keep Dad safe so that when he flies the helicopters and transport planes he doesn't have an accident. And, if You could, make Dad change his mind about my asking Alexis to show-and-tell. The kids have been teasing me a lot lately, and I just know it would help."

Judd felt an even bigger pain in his heart. His son was being teased at school? How come he hadn't told him about it?

"And God, I probably don't need Your help with this, but could You make sure if I do get to ask Alexis that she says she'll do it? She's a really nice lady. She talks to me like I'm a grown-up almost, and she lets me play with her iguana. Help Dad to see how important this is to me. Thanks again, God, for everything. Amen.''

Bryan scrambled into bed. Judd stepped into the hall, his throat closing with emotion. The innocent prayers of a little boy, spoken from the heart. Maybe it wouldn't be such a terrible thing to let him ask Alexis to go to school. At least if she turned him down Judd wouldn't have to carry that guilt, too.

Judd stepped into the room. ''Ready to sleep, sport?''

''I guess so.'' Bryan sounded subdued.

Judd took a deep breath and sat on the edge of the bed. ''Listen, buddy, if you want to ask Alexis if she'll go to show-and-tell, it's okay with me. But don't be disappointed if she says no. She's a busy person and—''

''You'll let me?'' Bryan shot out from under the covers and flung his arms around his father. ''Thanks, Dad, thanks!''

The child's warm little body felt so solid and sturdy beneath the cotton pajamas that Judd felt sorry when Bryan pulled away. He thought about all the times he had held Bryan as a baby, how comforting his warmth had been. The older he became, the less physical contact they seemed to have. The thought was an unsettling one. In a flash, Bryan was out of bed and running from the room.

''I got to go call her,'' he exclaimed.

''It's late. Wait until tomorrow,'' Judd advised, following him.

"I can't. She works such long hours I might not see her." He reached for the phone and began to dial. "I know she's home tonight. I saw her car."

Judd felt his stomach muscles tense as he listened to his son's end of the conversation with his neighbor.

Bryan put his hand over the receiver and said, "She said yes!" His eyes lit with excitement. "Can you pick her up and bring her to my school?"

Judd's lips tightened, and Bryan added, "I can't ask her to drive herself. I can't pay her or anything. Don't you think it would be the polite thing to do? You know, pick her up at the studio and then bring her back?"

Judd stifled a groan. He should have known it wouldn't work out so easily.

"I'll pick her up as long you promise never to ask for something like this again," he agreed.

"Never, honest."

Judd could recognize a phony promise when he saw one, but he let it slip by. The sooner this whole incident was over, the better.

Normally Alexis would have said no to any schoolboy's request that she be his show-and-tell object. She got enough attention as Katie Roberts. Besides, the producers of "Two Plus Two" didn't appreciate any of the cast leaving the set during rehearsals, which is what she needed to do to be a guest in Bryan's classroom.

Yet she had agreed to his request. She had left a

visitor's pass at the studio gate for Judd Shepard so that when he arrived he could come directly to the set.

She had just finished the opening scene when she saw Judd enter the sound stage. She was wearing an outfit from the Katie Roberts wardrobe, a matching two-piece skirt and blouse in a lime green with a black vest. She figured that some of Bryan's classmates would probably recognize the outfit, which would help her create the persona of the TV mom.

When Judd saw her approaching, his eyes narrowed. She wondered what she had done to produce such a frown.

"Good morning." She greeted him breezily, refusing to be intimidated by his brooding stare.

"Are you ready to go?" he asked impersonally.

"All set. This should be fun," she said enthusiastically. He didn't respond.

She followed him to the parking lot. He opened the passenger door for her before climbing in behind the steering wheel.

He wore cotton twill pants and a denim shirt. Tiny dark hairs protruded from the cuffs at his wrists, and a gold watch sparkled in the sunlight as he gripped the steering wheel. The vehicle had a standard transmission, which meant Judd had to use the stick shift on the floor frequently. His knuckles brushed against her cotton skirt, which rustled in the breeze.

The way he handled the vehicle gave Alexis the impression that he was in command. He exuded confidence. Considering he was a pilot, she guessed it shouldn't surprise her.

What *did* catch her off guard, however, was the way her stomach twittered whenever he cast a glance in her direction. There was something about sitting beside him that made her feel as if they were in an intimate setting. Maybe because the inside of the car smelled like leather and aftershave. A glance over her shoulder told her the reason. His bomber flight jacket lay sprawled across the back seat.

The uneasy silence that stretched between them needed to be broken. Alexis knew it, and she was certain he did, too.

Finally she said, "This is a first for me. I've never been someone's show-and-tell."

"I tried to discourage him from imposing on you, but he was determined to ask you."

"It's not an imposition," she lied.

"No, I suppose it's good for business."

She didn't like the implication. "That's not why I'm doing it."

He shrugged.

"I happen to think Bryan is a sweet boy, and he told me that he's been having problems getting along with some of the other kids in school, so I thought it might make things a little easier for him if I came as his guest."

Again he frowned, and she didn't understand why. Couldn't she say anything that wouldn't make him look as if he couldn't wait to get out of the car?

She tried another angle. "What did you think of the taping you saw?"

He kept his eyes on the road as he said, "Bryan enjoyed it."

"And you?"

"It was interesting," he said noncommittally.

There was another silence. She said, "I'm surprised you could take time away from your job to pick me up."

"With luck my beeper won't go off before we're through here," he said as he pulled into the school parking lot.

Alexis lowered her eyes and saw the pager fastened to his belt. "I could have driven myself."

Judd parked the car and turned off the engine. "You're Bryan's guest."

Alexis met his eyes, and her heart skipped a beat. She wanted him to have picked her up because it was what *he* wanted to do. The realization startled her, and she quickly averted her gaze, fumbling with the clasp on the seat belt.

When his fingers covered hers and released the belt, she felt a warm tingle of pleasure travel through her. "Thanks," she murmured, suddenly aware of a tension that had nothing to do with her being a TV star and him being a pilot.

As he had when she had entered the car, he opened her door for her and helped her out. As they walked side by side into the school building, Alexis felt the strangest sensation—like it was the most natural thing in the world for him to be at her side.

However, that was the last time he was at her side the rest of her visit. The fourth graders had an infinite number of questions. Her time in Bryan's classroom sped by, and before she knew it, she was leaving the school. As Judd had worried, his beeper had called him to an emergency. Alexis was driven to the studio by one of the school custodians, who chatted incessantly about his grandchildren who loved her TV program.

As Alexis returned to the set, she admitted there was only one reason she was disappointed. Judd hadn't been the one to drive her back.

The day had been particularly brutal, Judd thought, as he changed into swim trunks and grabbed a towel from the freshly folded stack on the counter. Upon arriving home, he had found a note from Mrs. Wahlstrom indicating she had taken Bryan to get an ice cream, which was fine with Judd. Since he was home earlier than usual and the sun was still very warm, the pool would feel mighty fine. Besides, it always felt good to swim away the tension that built in him during a busy run.

Judd padded barefoot to the pool and dropped his towel on the nearest lounge chair. A woman's voice made him glance over his shoulder.

"Mickey Mouse, very nice. He's always been one of my favorites, too."

He saw Alexis beside the pool, her scantily clad body spread across a Minnie Mouse beach towel, which could have been the twin to Judd's.

"It's Bryan's," Judd barked, quickly averting his eyes from her delectable figure.

"Of course," Alexis replied with amusement, seeming to enjoy his discomfiture. "I'm sure your beach towel is much more macho. Hercules, maybe?"

With a catlike curl she came to a sitting position and hugged her arms around her knees. The innocent gesture made her generous breasts swell to the brim of her suit. Judd felt a pinch in the pit of his stomach.

"Tell me," Alexis continued, unaware that Judd struggled for composure. "How come Bryan isn't with you?"

"He's not home." Judd didn't mean to sound harsh, but the sight of Alexis was doing unwelcome things to his insides. He was saved by a voice from across the pool.

"Hey, Alexis, is this true?" Walking toward them was Barry Wentworth, an aspiring actor who lived on the third floor and paid his rent by shampooing carpets, cleaning the stairs and foyers, watering plants and being a general maintenance man. It was obvious to Judd that, like Bryan, the young man was more than a little starstruck by the curvaceous Alexis.

"Oh, hi, Mr. Shepard," Barry added, as if he'd just noticed Judd.

"Is what true, Barry?" Alexis asked.

"This story in the newspaper." He held a tabloid between two fingers.

Alexis gave it a cursory glance and shrugged. "I doubt it. That's why I don't read tabloids. They're not noted for reporting stories accurately."

"Your picture's in here." He held up the photo of Alexis in the low-cut evening dress.

"That's the paparazzi for you. No matter where I go I risk having some photographer snap my picture." There was resignation and fatigue in her voice.

"Then this guy isn't your new boyfriend?" Barry asked hopefully.

"Oh, for heaven's sake!" Alexis laughed mirthlessly. "That guy is the college-age son of the man who directs 'Two Plus Two.' He was here visiting during a school break, and his dad wanted me to take him to a movie premier." She glanced again at the tabloid. "Actually, that photo will probably earn me points with the director. Now his son will have something to show his fraternity brothers."

"You are incredible, Alexis, do you know that?" The maintenance man tried to flatter her. "You take this sort of thing in your stride. Doesn't it upset you to see your picture splashed all over the newspapers?"

"Well, sure, it bothers me when the stories are inaccurate, but being photographed comes with the territory of being an actress. As a film student, you ought to know that. But no matter what that article implies, nothing's going on between me and Robbie Carlton."

Barry gave Judd a wink and said in an aside, "You could have fooled me." He sauntered away.

"I don't think he believed you," Judd remarked.

Alexis shrugged and stretched out again. "As if I care. He's a boy with delusions of grandeur. If he wants to believe gossip, that's his choice."

Gossip? Judd wondered if that's what it was. Those warning antennae of his were up again. Did he really believe Alexis was an innocent victim of the tabloids? Did she make a game of romance, as the papers wanted everyone to believe?

Judd dove into the pool and swam laps until he was exhausted. He had hoped that by the time he finished, she'd be gone. She wasn't. He climbed out of the pool, aware of her eyes on him.

When he reached for his towel, he noticed the tabloid she had tossed aside sat atop it. "You want this?" he asked, picking up the newspaper.

"You need to ask?" she drawled sarcastically.

He tossed the paper into a trash can, then grabbed his towel. Without drying himself, he started to walk away.

"Leaving so soon?" she asked.

"Bryan will be home in a few minutes," he replied, trying not to notice the interest in her eyes as he dabbed at the water dripping from his face.

"Tell him hi from me. And that he should come and feed Iggy one evening. I think that silly lizard misses him."

"Bryan's rather busy with school," he stated in a tone he knew she wouldn't misunderstand.

She sat up with a sigh. "Well, if he's *not* busy, he's always welcome." She gathered her things and stood to leave.

There was a challenge in her eyes that tempted Judd to continue the discussion. She wanted to argue with him. Only he'd already made up his mind. She was not going to get the better of either of the Shepard boys. So with a nod, he performed another difficult task. He walked away from Alexis Gordon.

CHAPTER FIVE

ALEXIS was tired as she parked in the garage. Although she had finished rehearsals early, it had been a trying day, and she was eager to get inside to the peace and quiet of her apartment.

She had taken but a couple of steps from the garage when Bryan Shepard rushed to greet her. "Hi, Katie—I mean, Alexis."

"Hi, yourself. What's up?" She couldn't help but smile at the youngster, so eager and enthusiastic.

"Did you know my birthday's coming up? I'm going to be ten on Saturday."

"You are? Why, that's an old man," she teased affectionately. "Do you think you'll be getting gray hair soon?"

Bryan grinned. "I checked today. None so far."

"Well, I hope you have a happy birthday, old man," Alexis said. She walked with him to the apartment building.

"Will you come? To my party, I mean? It's gonna be next Saturday at two o'clock. We're gonna to have lots of junk food and games and maybe even a treasure hunt! My dad said so."

The thought of Judd Shepard sent a funny little tingle through Alexis. The memory of Judd, dripping wet as he had climbed out of the pool, flashed in her mind, reminding her that her neighbor was one virile and physically fit man. Unfortunately he wanted nothing to do with her. Being at Bryan's party would mean spending the afternoon under Judd's glowering stare.

"I'm sorry, but I can't make it to your party, Bryan. It was sweet of you to ask me, though. Thanks."

All the enthusiasm in his face evaporated. "I guess my dad was right."

"Right about what?" Alexis couldn't stop herself from asking.

"He said you'd be too busy, but I didn't believe him. I thought you'd come." His little face looked as though it were about to collapse into tears.

"Your father told you I wouldn't come?"

Bryan nodded. "I'm sorry. I guess I should have listened to him and not asked you," he said dejectedly, and started to walk away.

"Bryan, wait!" Alexis called. "I might be able to change my plans for Saturday," she told him, ignoring the little voice in her head that warned her to stay away from the Shepards.

"You can?" Bryan beamed.

She nodded and smiled. "I can."

"Great! Let's go tell my dad!"

Alexis found herself being dragged through the hallway. Bryan's hand was warm and sticky in hers, as if he'd been clutching something sweet. He smelled of cinnamon and dust. Little-boy smells. Alexis rather liked it.

Bryan pushed open the door to his apartment and pulled her inside, yelling, "Dad, Dad!"

"What? Did you get hurt?" Judd burst into the room wearing nothing but a pair of jeans, which he'd obviously pulled on in a hurry, for they were open at the front. His chest was bare, broad and muscular. A fine cover of dark brown hair tapered to his waist—a waist Alexis didn't want to look at, since his zipper was undone.

She was unable to prevent the heat that spread through every inch of her body. It was one thing to see him in swim trunks at the pool, quite another to see him partially dressed in his own home.

At the sight of Alexis, he zipped his jeans. "Bryan, you should have told me you were bringing a guest back with you." There was no embarrassment on his face, but rather annoyance.

Alexis knew she was red to the roots of her hair. "Maybe it would be better if I came back another time," she said to Bryan

He grabbed her by the hand and tugged. "No, wait. We have to tell Dad the good news!"

Judd took a step closer to the two of them, eyeing Alexis suspiciously. "What news is that?"

"Bryan's invited me to his birthday party." The words nearly stuck in her throat. As an actress, she'd done love scenes with a lot of good-looking men wearing less clothing than Judd Shepard, but none had ever made her heart palpitate and her palms sweat.

"I told you she wouldn't say no, Dad." Bryan's

eyes glowed until he saw the look on his father's face. "It's all right, isn't it?"

The expression in Judd's eyes told Alexis it was definitely not all right, but his words were polite. "Of course. If you've invited her to be your guest, then she's welcome to come to the party."

Alexis noticed he didn't say *we* would like you to be *our* guest.

"I'm sure it will be a lot of fun," Alexis stated smoothly.

"See? She's not too busy!" Bryan pointed out to his father.

Judd said, "I tried to explain to Bryan that people in show business have busy schedules."

"Which is why you didn't want him asking me?"

"I didn't want him to be disappointed if you couldn't make it."

"Maybe next time check with me first," Alexis retorted sweetly, with an underlying acerbity. "You see, I know my own schedule."

Judd's eyes narrowed. However, Bryan was oblivious to the tension between them. He was bouncing around the room chanting, "She's coming! She's coming. Katie's coming!"

Judd's voice was sharp as he said, "He can't seem to keep the two of you straight—actress and make-believe mom. He thinks you're the maternal type."

"Maybe he knows me better than you think he does," she said coyly, disliking his implication. "I guess you'll just have to wait and see." And with a lift of her chin, she said goodbye to Bryan and left, breathing a sigh of relief when she was in the hallway and away from the penetrating gaze of Judd Shepard.

"I got two tickets to the Dodgers game for Saturday. How about you taking that kid across the hall?" Ray suggested as he and Alexis ate dinner at a quiet restaurant not far from the studio.

"Give it up, Ray," Alexis warned him, then took a sip of her white wine. "I told you. If I do anything with Bryan Shepard, it won't be for promotional reasons."

"I didn't say you had to do this as a publicity stunt."

"So there wouldn't be a photographer waiting at the ballpark?" She raised one eyebrow inquisitively.

"There are always photographers hanging around the stadium. Baseball makes the news," he reminded her.

"Well, I don't want to be a part of baseball's news and I especially don't want Bryan to get caught up in any publicity stunt." She attacked her pasta salad with a vengeance.

"I know you went to the kid's school."

She didn't respond.

"Why are you so uptight when it comes to this kid?"

"I'm not. I just get tired of not being able to have any privacy."

"You should know that you're going to be in next week's *Gossip Galore*." His dark brows knit together.

Alexis dropped her fork. "Again?"

He nodded. "I think they must have a vendetta against you."

Gossip Galore was a tabloid that regularly printed inaccurate stories about Alexis. Sometimes she felt as if they were publishing a day-by-day account of her personal life. When they had crossed the line and involved her family in their shabby journalism, she had seen an attorney with the intention of suing. She soon discovered, however, that litigation wouldn't stop the tabloid's relentless pursuit of her.

Alexis sighed. "Why can't they just leave me alone?" She shoved aside her pasta salad, her appetite deserting her.

"That's why it's important that we work on your image. They don't know you the way I do. Just because you're drop-dead gorgeous and single, they assume you're a vain, selfish woman who doesn't care about anything but her career."

"You're right. They don't know me," she said somberly.

"I wish you'd reconsider letting me get you some press with this kid." When she began to protest, he held up his hands to silence her. "I know. You don't want to use him, but it's not using him. What you're doing for him—being his friend—is genuine caring on your part. The public would like to know that aspect of your personality."

She swirled the wine in her glass, studying it as though it were a crystal ball that held the key to her future. "That might be true, but I'm not willing to take that chance. The tabloids could just as easily exploit my relationship with Bryan."

Ray sighed in frustration. "All right. Will you take the boy to the Dodgers game if I promise I won't send the photographer?"

She shook her head. "I can't. It's his birthday, and his dad is having a party for him."

"At the apartment complex?" he asked with interest.

She eyed him suspiciously. "No, and I'm not going to tell you where it is."

He gave her a wounded look. "I can't believe you don't trust me."

"It isn't a question of trust, Ray. I know you are a darn good publicist, and if you thought you were helping my career by doing something, you would do it—whether I wanted you to or not."

"That's what you pay me to do," he said with a sheepish grin.

"Well, this Saturday I need you to be my friend, not my publicist."

She could see he wasn't happy with her request, but he didn't argue. One thing Alexis didn't need was for Judd Shepard to think she was using his son to further her career. She would attend Bryan's birthday party, as his next door neighbor, not as Katie Roberts, the perfect TV mom, and if there were going to be any photographs, she wanted them to be taken by the guest of honor's father, not the paparazzi.

Although the party room at the exclusive apartment complex was available to all tenants, Judd took the advice of Peggy, the party planner, to move the birthday celebration to a pizza parlor that had a banquet room with pinball machines and video games. As soon as the first of the partygoers arrived, he could see that it was a good idea. The boys didn't hide their excitement at the chance to play the video games.

Judging by the squeals of delight and the laughter, Judd concluded the party was a success. Peggy proved to be worthy of her fee, leading the rambunctious group of boys in several games as well as overseeing the refreshments. To Judd's surprise, after the initial excitement over Alexis Gordon's appearance, the boys paid little attention to the TV star. At least everyone but Bryan did.

While his friends plunked their complimentary quarters into the video games, he was content to sit beside Alexis at the banquet table until the pizza arrived. Judd wished he'd play with the other boys, but no amount of encouragement was going to get his son to leave the TV star's side.

When the pizza was served, Peggy managed to corral the boys and get them seated. Judd would have liked to sit away from Alexis, but as Bryan's father, he needed to be at the head of the table. So he took the chair next to Bryan, who sat directly across from Alexis.

If Judd thought the boys didn't care about the make-believe mom, he was proved wrong. Several boys battled to get the chairs closest to her. A small skirmish erupted. Alexis stood and faced the group.

"I'll tell you what. Since it's Bryan's birthday, I'll sit next to him while we eat the pizza. But when cake is served, I'll move to the other end of the table. All right?"

All but Bryan looked happy. Judd was about to lean over and tell his son he couldn't expect to be the center of attention for the entire party when Alexis beat him to it.

"I know it's your birthday, Bryan, but you are the host of the party and you need to consider your guests' feelings. You want them to have a good time, right?"

He nodded.

"Good." She placed her hand over his and gave it a squeeze. "You're such a thoughtful young man. That's one of the things I like about you." Then she flashed him a smile that had Bryan practically melting in his chair.

Not that Judd blamed him. That smile wasn't even directed at him, and he could feel its power. It was like being outdoors on a gray day and having the sun chase away the clouds.

After the last piece of pizza had been consumed and the cake and ice cream were but a memory in everyone's minds, it was time for Bryan to open his presents. Everyone gathered in a circle on the floor. Judd and Alexis stood outside the ring of boys, as did Peggy.

"Oh, boy" and "neat" were exclamations heard often as Bryan tore the wrapping from his birthday packages. Bryan saved two presents for the very end. One was from Alexis, the other from Judd.

Ever since Bryan had been old enough to handle the tiny pieces of model airplane kits, father and son had worked side by side putting them together. In their collection were many fighter planes, as well as replicas of some of the earliest passenger planes. It was a hobby they shared and one they hadn't given much time to since Carol had died.

For this birthday Judd had looked high and low to find a model of the North American Mustang. It hadn't been easy, but after many long-distance phone calls he had finally found a hobby shop that could fill his order for the miniature fighter plane.

Judd watched with his enthusiasm held firmly in check while Bryan opened the package. Just as he suspected, Bryan's eyes lit up at the sight of the model airplane kit. "Cool! A Mustang! Thanks, Dad." However, to Judd's dismay, the box was quickly cast aside as Bryan reached for the gift from Alexis.

He removed the glossy paper from the package, his cheeks glowing, his eyes wide. When he lifted the lid from the box, he squealed in delight.

"Wow! A 'Two Plus Two' cap!"

It was a navy blue baseball cap with the logo of the TV show embroidered across the front. All the boys huddled closer as Bryan set it on his head and preened for them. "This is the best present ever!"

"Man, you're lucky," one boy said enviously.

"I want one!" The comment was repeated often.

Bryan looked at Alexis. "You can't buy these, can you?"

"No, they're only for the cast and crew," she answered, which made Bryan's eyes gleam even brighter.

"Gee, thanks, Ka—I mean Alexis," he said, getting up to throw his arms around her waist in an affectionate display of emotion.

Judd watched as Peggy gathered discarded wrapping paper and the boys returned to the video games. Even Bryan took a turn, the "Two Plus Two" cap squarely on his head. As soon as the mess had been cleared, Peggy left. Judd turned his attention to collecting the birthday gifts.

"The party was great," Alexis told him, toying with a piece of ribbon. "I had a good time. Thank you."

"You should have thanked Peggy before she left. She made all the arrangements," Judd said testily.

"Well, you made a good choice in choosing the party planning service. Bryan's lucky he has you for a father."

He didn't need her compliments, nor did he want them, which was why he was abrupt as he said,

"That's not what you were saying a few weeks ago." He spread his arms and motioned to the video games and the party balloons. "Is this what you think makes a good father? Someone who can buy the trimmings and entertainment?"

He watched all traces of friendliness disappear from her face. She folded her arms and faced him squarely.

"What is it with you? Do you get pleasure out of being sour? I was simply trying to tell you that you did a nice thing for your son, and all I get is grief. Since the day I met Bryan you've gone out of your way to let me know that you don't want me around. Well, as far as I'm concerned you can take that lousy attitude of yours and go stand in front of a mirror."

Judd watched her grab her purse from the table and march over to Bryan. She gave him and each of the boys a hug, then waved goodbye. As he watched her slim figure leave the room, remorse washed over Judd. He had behaved very badly, and all because Bryan had liked the gift from Alexis better than he had liked Judd's.

To make matters worse, all the way home Bryan sang their neighbor's praises, pointing out the nice things she had said to all the boys. When his son said, "It was the next best thing to having Mom there," Judd felt as if someone had slugged him in the stomach.

What would Carol have thought about Judd's behavior at the party? Later that evening, after Bryan fell asleep, Judd knew what he had to do. He slipped quietly out of the apartment and took the few steps to Alexis's door.

Alexis was curled up liked a pretzel on the sofa with a large patchwork quilt draped across her lap when the doorbell rang. With a sigh of frustration, she stuck the needle into the fabric and gently eased the quilt from her lap onto the sofa. Barefoot, she padded across the thick carpet to the door.

When she glanced through the peephole she was tempted to pretend she wasn't home. Judd Shepard was the last person she wanted to see this evening. After their scene at Bryan's birthday party, she didn't care if she ever saw the man again.

She paused with her hand on the doorknob, and the bell chimed for a second time. She took another look at him, and she couldn't ignore the familiar tingle of pleasure she felt whenever they were in the same room. She swung open the door.

"Need to borrow some sugar?" she asked sassily.

"No, I need to apologize. May I come in?"

She stepped aside and gestured for him to enter. As soon as she had closed the door, she faced him, her arms folded across her chest.

He rubbed a hand across the back of his neck and sighed. "I behaved badly this afternoon at Bryan's party, and I'm sorry. I'm afraid I've been operating on a short fuse all week long. I know that doesn't excuse my behavior, but it's about the only reason I can think of for acting so rudely."

"Apology accepted," she said quietly, fighting the urge to smooth the lines of stress and fatigue from his face.

"Instead of ragging on you, I should have been thanking you. It was nice of you to come to Bryan's party, and I know it meant a lot to him having you there," he said sincerely.

"I enjoyed the party. It's not often I get to see cake being flung across the table," she said with a grin.

He returned the smile. "I know what you mean. They were a rowdy bunch, weren't they?"

Alexis rolled her eyes. "Thank goodness for Peggy. She's really good at her job."

"She told me she has three boys of her own," Judd remarked.

"Aha."

An awkward silence stretched between them. Alexis said, "Would you like something to drink? Coffee? A soda?"

"No, I really shouldn't stay. Bryan's asleep. I need to get back," he answered.

She nodded. "Maybe another time. Oh—before you go, I have something for you." She walked to the bookcase on the far wall of the living room and pulled a pocket-size red convertible from one of the shelves. "This must have fallen out of Bryan's pocket when he was here feeding Iggy. I found it on the floor."

As Judd walked over to get the toy from her, he

noticed the unfinished quilt draped over the sofa. "That's your handiwork?"

"Uh-huh. It's for my younger sister. She's getting married in August."

"And you're making her a quilt?"

"Yes. Is there something unusual about that?"

He shrugged. "I guess not." He tugged on his ear. "I guess I never would have pictured you as the type to be at a quilting bee."

"I don't go to quilting bees. I'm just doing something that I enjoy."

Noticing the embroidery hoop on the end table, he said, "I haven't seen one of those since I was a kid and my grandmother would put fancy initials on all the sheets and pillowcases."

"That's where I learned to embroider—from my grandmother. She also taught me how to quilt." She could feel him staring at her. "What's wrong?"

"Nothing," he admitted. "It's just that I didn't expect the star of a big hit like 'Two Plus Two' would be sitting home on a Saturday night with needle and thread for companions."

Alexis thought admiration flashed in those dark brown eyes, if only for a few seconds. "Then I guess you learned something, didn't you? Appearances can be deceptive—and not always in a negative way," she told him.

"You think I've misjudged you?"

Alexis felt her mouth go dry as his eyes glinted

with masculine interest. "I think you haven't given me much of a chance to show you who I really am."

"And who is the real Alexis? The woman who on her day off eats pizza and plays video games with a group of ten-year-old boys, then comes home to spend Saturday night sewing a wedding quilt?" The interest continued to radiate from his dark eyes.

"You sound as if that couldn't be me."

"It doesn't exactly fit—"

"With the image the press has created for me?" she interrupted, thrusting her palms in the air. "I know that. My public persona has been painted by a handful of newspapers and magazines who want to make me into something I'm not." She spoke ardently.

"I'm beginning to realize that." He caressed her with his eyes, sending her heartbeat up a notch.

"I'm just an ordinary citizen, and I'd like for you to treat me the same way you do Jenny or Barry or any of the other tenants in this building," she told him huskily.

"But I don't want to think of them the same way I think of you," he said, his eyes darkening.

"Why is that? Because I happen to be an actress on TV?"

"No, because of this." He moved closer and drew her against him in an intimate gesture that left her in little doubt of what he was about to do.

Then his lips brushed hers in a sensuous exploration. A tremor of desire vibrated through her, followed by a wave of warmth as his mouth moved over hers. She clung to him, wanting the kiss to go on forever, but all too soon he was reluctantly pulling away.

From the look on his face Alexis was certain he was just as surprised by the urgency of their kiss as she was.

"I don't think Barry would appreciate that," he said, showing her he had a sense of humor hidden beneath that rugged exterior. Then he flashed her a wicked grin and walked to the door.

Alexis could only stare at him, stunned by her feelings. She struggled to think of a clever comeback, but her lips appeared to be paralyzed from one very hot kiss.

He paused. "Bryan was right about you. You are one very special lady, Alexis Gordon."

Special was exactly how she felt as she sat again with her quilt. Long after he was gone, she thought about Judd Shepard. If he truly did think she was special, did it mean he would no longer object to her friendship with Bryan?

As she prepared for bed that evening, she knew that as much as she enjoyed the ten-year-old's company, the Shepard she really wanted to get to spend more time with was Judd.

CHAPTER SIX

TEN-THIRTY at night was no time to be grocery shopping, Judd mused as he examined a head of wilted lettuce. The rest of the produce didn't look much better, but he supposed he'd better bring home the items on the list Mrs. Wahlstrom had given him. It was times like this that he really missed having a wife. No matter how hard Mrs. Wahlstrom tried to keep the household running smoothly, she couldn't replace Carol.

Judd pushed thoughts of his wife from his mind. It never failed. Fatigue made him more susceptible to the loneliness that haunted him, and he was extremely tired tonight.

His steps grew heavier as he trudged down the aisles looking for cereal, milk, crackers and cherry pie filling. The other patrons of the store were as exhausted-looking as he, and mostly male. This must be the time of night men decide they are hungry, Judd thought, wishing he'd never offered to do the shopping.

Only one line was open when Judd reached the front of the store. Two bored men leaned against their carts, waiting their turn with the cashier. The first, a service station attendant with the name Al sewn over

97

the pocket of his coveralls, was paging through one of the tabloids from the rack next to the counter. When it was his turn to put his groceries on the conveyor belt, he slipped the tabloid into place on the rack and spoke to the man behind him, an overweight biker wearing a leather vest and sporting tattoos on practically every inch of exposed skin.

"I normally don't read those things, but that one caught my eye because of the babe on the front," Al announced as he set several cans of dog food on the counter.

Judd couldn't help but hear and glanced at the cover of the tabloid. The babe the man referred to was none other than his neighbor. Alexis Gordon wore a different dress in this picture—one with a slit up the side and straps that looked more like threads of spaghetti than a support system.

She was with a different man, as well. Blond, this time, with a square jaw, piercing blue eyes and a belligerent look that said, "Take another photo of us and I'll pound your head in." Alexis looked very comfortable with her human pit bull, Judd observed. She appeared to enjoy the thick hand hovering protectively at her slim waist.

"She's a looker, isn't she?" the biker remarked, picking up the tabloid and adding it to his collection of items. "I've seen her on that TV show, and I can tell you one thing. None of my friends' moms looked like that when I was a kid."

"Ain't that the truth?" Al asked with a cynical

smile. "But then she's only a make-believe mother. Just look at her. She ain't exactly the motherly type. It's gotta all be an act."

The biker chuckled. "Yeah. I read somewhere she hates kids."

"Just goes to show you what a good actress she is," Al remarked with a nasty grin.

"Personally, I don't care whether she likes kids or not," the biker stated. "A woman that good-looking would be wasted being some kid's mother."

"According to those tabloids, she's out with a different guy every week. She's the love 'em and leave 'em type, if you ask me."

Judd tried to tune out their conversation, but it wasn't easy to ignore their voices. The service station attendant continued. "Yes, sir, I watch all those talk shows about the stars. That Alexis is one big heart-breaker."

Finally the cashier spoke up. "She *is* single, you know."

"Oh, yeah," the biker answered with a lecherous grin Judd would have liked to smack right off his face. "Have you ever really looked at her legs? Being a mom on that TV show, she probably doesn't show them off, but I saw her in a bikini once, and vava-voom!"

Judd knew what was said about Alexis's legs was true. He remembered his reaction when he'd seen her in a bathing suit. The memory was enough to cause him to feel warm. He picked up a *TV Guide* and began flipping through it, not wanting to think another thought about Alexis Gordon.

After what seemed like an eternity, it was Judd's turn with the cashier. As she scanned his groceries, Judd thought about the lack of privacy Alexis or any celebrity had. It would be abhorrent to him to have his personal life discussed and speculated about so casually. How did she stand it?

Then he shrugged. Stand it? She was the one who had chosen it! Surely she'd known the price of fame and sought it anyway. Was he a fool for thinking there was a warm, compassionate woman beneath the fancy trimmings of the television star? Of one thing he was certain. She had a way of seducing men. He was proof of that. He didn't even like the woman, yet he had kissed her.

At the memory of that kiss, he felt his chest tighten. He certainly had liked kissing Alexis Gordon. But then why shouldn't he? She was a beautiful woman, and it had been a long, long time since he had felt the urge to…

He closed his eyes and forced the thought from his mind. He was a single dad with responsibilities. Flirting with his neighbor was not one of them. What he needed to concentrate on was making more time for his son, something that was pointed out to him when he arrived home.

To Judd's dismay, Bryan was not in bed.

"You have school tomorrow. What are you doing up?" he asked his son.

"I wanted to talk to you."

Judd felt a wave of guilt wash over him.

Together they put away the groceries, Bryan chattering like a magpie, Judd listening and realizing that his schedule had been much too hectic lately with too little time for his son. Unfortunately, he didn't see any time in the near future that things would ease up. One of his pilots was on vacation and another's wife was scheduled for knee surgery. That meant Judd would take up the slack.

"Well, will you, Dad?"

Judd turned to Bryan. "Sorry, son, my mind must have drifted off. I didn't hear what you said."

Bryan gave his father an impatient look. "I said, will you come to the open house at school with me on Tuesday? It's going to be great. We've been working on art collages and we're going to have our science projects on display. I'm not supposed to tell, but we even made presents for everybody who comes. Cool, huh?"

"Very cool," Judd said carefully, suddenly aware of a tightness in his midsection. Tuesday was the day he'd promised to cover for Ted while his wife had surgery.

"You'll be there, right, Dad?" Bryan looked at him hopefully.

Judd searched for the words. Before he said anything, however, Bryan spoke.

"You're not coming, are you?" His face twisted in disappointment.

"I want to, but we're going to be short two pilots next week."

"Well, hire another one!" Bryan demanded, wrapping his arms across his chest stubbornly. "You never come to anything at school anymore. Ever since Mom died, everything's changed. All you do is work, work, work! Now I'm going to be the only kid at open house without a parent!" he declared in a near scream as he ran from the room.

Judd rubbed the back of his neck. How could he make his son understand? People's lives depended on him being able to fly a plane at a moment's notice.

For the second time that night, Judd felt the loneliness Carol's death had created. Would he never stop missing her? At least if she were alive, Bryan would have one of his parents at the open house.

But she wasn't here, and once again Judd had to be both mother and father to Bryan. It was a job he wasn't doing very well.

On Tuesday afternoon, Judd sat with the invitation to the Sunny Hollow Elementary School Open House in front of him on his desk. He drew a line through the fifth name on a list of substitute pilots he routinely called when he needed extra help. So far no one could work that evening.

Judd was down to the final phone call. If pilot number six wasn't available, Judd was going to have to accept the inevitable. He wasn't going to be able to attend the open house.

The sixth pilot wasn't home, so Judd left a message, then hung up the receiver with a thud. There was nothing to do but call Mrs. Wahlstrom and tell her to have Bryan catch a ride to school with his friend Andy.

To Judd's relief, the substitute pilot returned his call and agreed to fill in. Judd would be a few minutes late, but at least he would be able to attend. He couldn't wait to see Bryan's reaction when he walked into the school. There was nothing more rewarding for a father than to be able to chase away the sadness on his son's face.

Only when Judd arrived at the school, Bryan did not look the least bit unhappy. Actually, he looked pretty pleased. And it didn't take Judd long to discover the reason. Alexis Gordon was peering over the science projects, acting as if they were the most interesting thing she'd seen all day.

As if he could hear the words of the men in the grocery store, Judd looked at her legs. They were covered by the trousers of the red pantsuit she wore. As usual, she looked beautiful, and he felt the familiar response his body made whenever they were in the same room. It was not unlike the exhilaration he felt whenever he successfully landed a plane in difficult weather conditions.

As if she sensed him staring at her, she turned and smiled. Placing a hand on Bryan's shoulder, she directed his attention to the classroom entrance where Judd stood.

Bryan hurried over to grab his father by the hand. "Dad! You came!"

"Yes, I was able to get someone after all," Judd explained, allowing his son to drag him to the long table next to the windows where the science projects were displayed.

"Come look at what I made." Bryan stopped next to Alexis. "Are you ready to see it?" he asked eagerly.

Judd nodded, scanning the name tags in search of his son's.

"It's not down there," Bryan chided him. "It's up there." He lifted his eyes to the ceiling, pointing with his finger.

Judd glanced up and saw a mobile of the solar system dangling overhead. "So that's why you needed the wire and string," he mused.

"What do you think? Is it cool, Dad?"

Judd ruffled his hair affectionately. "It's cool."

"Alexis thought so, too." Again he pulled Judd by the hand. "Come on. You got to see my collage."

Judd allowed him to lead him to the opposite end of the classroom. A frieze of artwork trimmed the chalkboard.

"Can you guess which one is mine?" Bryan asked with a sly grin.

Judd surveyed the pictures created from bits and pieces of newspapers and magazines. Knowing how much Bryan enjoyed baseball, he pointed to one that pictured a catcher's mitt made out of snapshots of athletes in action.

"No way," Bryan told him.

Judd continued to look. When he saw one that was a large television with names of prime time TV programs jumbled in the square where the screen should have been, his stomach plummeted. He raised one eyebrow and looked at Bryan, who to Judd's relief shook his head.

"You're getting closer," Bryan told him as he continued to walk past the pictures.

Finally, he found what he knew had to be his son's creative work. Large red letters said Emergency across the top of a collection of pictures depicting rescue events. Included was a photo of a patient being transported onto a helicopter.

"Do you like it?" Bryan asked as Judd's eyes lingered on the glossy clippings comprising the bigger picture.

Judd had to swallow the lump in his throat. "I do. You did a good job."

"I had to go through a lot of magazines to find the right pictures," Bryan explained as Judd examined the collage.

The teacher announced that the program was about to begin. All students needed to report to the auditorium.

"Oops. I gotta go," Bryan told his dad. He turned to Alexis and said, "Don't forget. I'm on the left side of the stage." Before Judd could ask him what was going on, he disappeared into the rush of his class-mates pouring out the door.

"He's rather excited, isn't he?" Alexis com-mented. "His class is reciting the Declaration of Independence."

As the parents filed out of the room, Judd said, "I see. I guess we'd better head to the auditorium, then."

"You were surprised to find me here, weren't you?" Alexis commented as they followed the crowd of people down the hallway.

"Bryan didn't tell me he had invited you."

"Oh, he didn't invite me," she corrected him.

"Then he must have dropped some pretty obvious hints," Judd said wryly.

"No, he didn't."

"Then why did you come?"

"Because I found him sitting behind the garage crying."

That brought Judd to a stop. He faced her and asked, "What are you talking about?"

"Apparently his friend Andy was supposed to give him a ride, but he got sick at the last minute and couldn't go. When I came home, I found Bryan be-hind the garage, quite upset. He said you were work-ing, that Mrs. Wahlstrom couldn't give him a ride and he had no way of getting to his open house at school."

"So you offered to take him," he concluded, re-suming his walk.

"It seemed like the neighborly thing to do."

"It was a very kind thing to do. Thank you," Judd said sincerely.

"You're welcome."

Any further discussion on the subject was preempted as they reached the auditorium and tried to find a place to sit. They sat close to the front on the left side so they would be able to get a good look at Bryan.

There was a variety of performances including musical numbers, poetry and dramatic presentations, none of which lasted more than a few minutes. At the very end of the program, the students passed out tiny flags, the special gifts Bryan had mentioned. Before long, Judd found himself ushering Bryan and Alexis out of the school and into the parking lot.

"Can we stop and get an ice cream?" Bryan asked as they walked Alexis to her car. "And please don't say, 'No it's a school night.'"

Judd didn't want to refuse his son's request. "All right. We'll stop for ice cream."

"Can Alexis come, too?"

Judd nearly said, "I'm sure she's busy," but remembered how upset she had been when he had spoken on her behalf before. So he turned to her and asked, "Would you like to join us?"

She looked as if she might say no, but then she smiled and said, "Sure. Where are you going?"

Before Judd could make a suggestion, Bryan said, "DJ's? Please?" He turned to Alexis and said, "They make the best ice cream pizzas there."

"Um, sounds good," she agreed.

"And we can take it home with us. That way we can eat the leftovers tomorrow." Bryan's eyes gleamed.

So Judd let his son pick out the ice cream pizza of his choice—a chocolate, caramel and peanut confection they decided would taste best in the familiar surroundings of home.

"Good choice, Bryan," Alexis commended him as they sat at the counter that separated the kitchen from the dining room. "I'll have to remember DJ's when my sweet tooth aches."

While they ate they talked about the open house and the start of summer break, only a couple of weeks away. Bryan had barely finished his slice when his eyes began to droop.

Seeing him yawn, Alexis said, "I should get going. Bryan's tired."

He immediately straightened. "No, I'm not."

Judd gave him a look that said he knew better. "You can get yourself ready for bed. Alexis can stay and finish her ice cream."

"Okay," he reluctantly agreed. "Thanks for taking me to school tonight, Alexis. I'm really glad you came."

"I'm glad I did, too." She watched as he gave his father a hug before scurrying off to his room.

"I want to thank you again for coming to Bryan's rescue this evening." Judd leaned back, his head angled in a way that reminded Alexis of Bryan.

"I'm just glad I was home early enough to help out."

"You seem to be doing that a lot lately…helping out," Judd remarked, his look guarded.

She couldn't tell if he were pleased or unhappy about it. She had thought he had let go of the reservations he had about her. Now she wasn't so sure.

"Is there a reason I shouldn't?" she asked cautiously.

A shadow of worry crossed his face, but he said, "No, there really isn't. Bryan is very fond of you."

She knew there was a lingering doubt in his mind. "But you'd rather he not spend so much time with me, right?"

"I don't want him to make a nuisance of himself."

"I'll let you know if he does," she assured him. "As I told you, I enjoy being with him. He's very sweet."

"You must have better things to do with your time."

"I think it's for me to decide, don't you?"

He shifted uncomfortably on his chair.

"Look, if you still believe I'm some kind of bad influence on your son, then say so. But don't make decisions about how I spend my time." She shoved her empty plate aside, dabbed at her mouth with a napkin then stood to leave. He jumped up to stop her.

"I don't think you're a bad influence on my son." He reached for her hands and held them. "I'm just a concerned parent who's a little worried that his son might be getting too emotionally attached to someone for all the wrong reasons.''

''You think he only sees me as a television star?''

''He *is* one of Katie Roberts's biggest fans,'' Judd said soberly.

''Yes, I realize that, but I think if you talk to him you'll see that Alexis Gordon is the person he wants to spend time with, not Katie Roberts.''

''I can understand that.'' His eyes darkened as he studied her.

''You can?''

''Yes, because there's not a man alive who wouldn't enjoy spending time with you.''

She found herself short of breath. ''Is that what you think?''

''It's what I know. I've seen the effect you have on boys—big and small.''

Prickles of awareness traveled up and down her arms. She gently eased her hands out of his. ''I don't know if I should take that as a compliment or not.''

He reached out and traced the contour of her cheek with his index finger. ''You're a lovely person, Alexis, inside and out. Not many women in your profession would have made the time to do the things you've done for Bryan.''

Warmth slowly spread throughout her body at his touch. ''Maybe I'm not like most women in my profession.''

''I'd like to think that.'' He tipped her face with his hand, studying her.

She trembled in anticipation of the kiss she knew was only moments away. But it never happened, for Bryan came rushing into the kitchen.

"Dad, I forgot to tell you. We're going on a field trip to the science museum next week and I need you to sign the permission slip." He shoved a piece of paper in front of Judd.

A twinkle lit his eyes as he looked from his dad to Alexis.

"I can go, can't I?"

"Sure." While Judd searched for a pen, Alexis walked toward the door.

"I'm going to say good-night," she announced, wishing she didn't feel as if her face was flaming.

"She doesn't have to go, does she, Dad?" Bryan asked.

"Oh, but I do," Alexis answered before Judd could reply. She had already spent far too much time with the Shepard boys. Unless she was careful, she was in danger of losing her heart to both of them.

CHAPTER SEVEN

"Sit still or I'll turn around and take you right back home." Mrs. Kane frowned in the rearview mirror at the two boys bouncing in the back seat. "Have you got your seat belts on?"

Buckles could be heard snapping into place as both boys grew very still. "Please don't turn around," Bryan begged. "Katie—I mean Alexis is expecting us at the beach."

"Two By Two" was filming on location, and much to Bryan's delight, Alexis had made sure he could come watch. What was even better was that he was able to bring his friend Andy. Bryan saw it as a good sign. If she didn't really like him, she wouldn't have arranged everything.

What had surprised Bryan was that his dad hadn't fought the idea. Ever since the night Alexis had come to his open house, his dad hadn't complained about him spending too much time with her. Bryan hoped it meant what Andy said was true, that his dad had the hots for Alexis.

Bryan had seen his dad touch Alexis's cheek and put his face close to hers. And the look that had been on his face that night—well, he wasn't sure what it meant, but it was the same old sappy look he had seen in his dad's eyes when he used to kiss his mom.

Bryan smiled at the memory. It would be so cool if his dad did get the hots for Katie. Because if they got married, she would be his *real* mother. He wouldn't have to watch her on television anymore— but of course, he would, because he really liked "Two Plus Two."

The closer they got to the beach, the more his excitement grew. Trucks of camera equipment and the stars' trailers came into view.

"There's her trailer!" Bryan crowed, pressing his nose against the window. "This is cool!"

"Where am I supposed to go?" Mrs. Kane asked, slowing for a traffic sign.

"Just drop us off at the entrance," Bryan said importantly. "Alexis said she'd watch for us."

And she was true to her word, sitting on the top step of her trailer. Already in costume and makeup, she was working the crossword puzzle from the morning paper. She looked very motherly indeed.

Mrs. Kane assured Alexis that she would be back to pick up Andy by six o'clock. "You be good," she warned the two of them, wagging her finger in their faces.

The boys didn't even turn to watch Mrs. Kane drive away. Instead, they each took one of Alexis's hands and walked to where the taping was to take place. In the episode being filmed, the Roberts family was spending the day at the beach. She led them to a roped-off area.

"You two will have to stay behind this rope, all right?"

Both boys nodded eagerly and watched as the cast of "Two Plus Two" gathered around the director. The taping went so smoothly, it seemed like minutes passed rather than hours when Mrs. Kane returned.

"Do I have to go already?" Andy whined. "It's not fair. Bryan gets to stay."

Bryan knew his moment had come. He looked at his friend's disconsolate face and then at Alexis, who was brushing sand from her skirt as she prepared for the final scene. A sly, thoughtful expression crossed his youthful features. "Maybe I should go home with you. Would that make you feel better?"

"You'd leave now?" Andy gawked in disbelief.

"Isn't your father planning to pick you up?" Mrs. Kane reminded him.

"It's okay," Bryan said brightly. "I can call him and tell him he doesn't have to come."

"Can Bryan eat dinner at our house?" Andy asked his mother.

"If you're sure it's okay with your father," she said to Bryan, who nodded eagerly.

"Wait here and I'll be right back." He ran to Alexis. "Thanks a lot for letting us come to the taping."

"You're leaving?" She glanced to where Andy

stood next to his mother and waved. "Isn't your father coming to pick you up?"

"Yeah, but I decided to go home with Andy. When my dad gets here, tell him I'm having supper with the Kanes and there's no hurry to pick me up, okay?" Before Alexis could respond, he turned and ran to the car, a satisfied grin on his face.

Alexis waved and headed for her trailer, where she changed into a pair of shorts and a sweatshirt. She had just finished work when Judd arrived on the set. He sauntered toward her.

"I suppose my son has stars in his eyes and I'm going to have to drag him away from here," he said with a half-grin.

"I don't think so. In fact, he left early."

"He *left?*" A frown creased his brow. "He was supposed to wait for me."

"He told me to tell you that he went home with Andy and was going to have dinner there. Oh, yes, and that there was no hurry to pick him up." Alexis released the clip that had held her blond hair in place during the taping, her fingers acting like a comb as she shook it free.

"Was he sick?" Judd asked.

"No. Why do you ask?"

"Because that's the only reason I can think of that he could be coaxed into leaving early."

"No one had to do any coaxing," she said with a chuckle. "He didn't appear to be feeling ill at all.

Actually, he looked rather excited about getting to eat dinner with Andy.''

"Well, that makes no sense whatsoever.''

Alexis shot him a puzzled look.

"The reason I came to pick him up instead of having Mrs. Kane take him home was so we could have a picnic supper on the beach,'' Judd explained.

"Maybe he forgot?''

"It was *his* idea. He's the one who wanted me to stop at the deli and pick up a couple of submarine sandwiches so we could watch the sun set over the water.'' Realization dawned in Judd's eyes. "Why that little…'' He trailed off in disbelief.

"Excuse me?'' Alexis looked startled.

"Bryan, the little schemer. He left early for a *reason*. He had me bring enough food for two people, and then he conveniently left with Andy.''

Alexis was catching Judd's drift. "You mean he *wanted* you to be here alone? You aren't suggesting that he's trying to play matchmaker, are you?''

"I don't know, but I do plan to find out.'' Judd's expression was grim as he rubbed the back of his neck and stared at the water as it hit the sand, then rolled away.

"What are you going to do?''

He looked at her and chuckled. "You can relax. I'm not going to lock him in his room and feed him bread and water.''

"I didn't think you would,'' she said. "If he did do as you suspect—you know, try to set up a dinner for two—well, it's not exactly a criminal offense, is it?''

"No, just another reason he shouldn't be spending so much time with you.''

"You think this is my fault?''

"Ever since he met you he's been fantasizing about having you for a mother.''

"Considering his circumstances, is that so unexpected? I mean, he *is* a motherless boy, and I play a mom on television. I'm sure there are lots of children like Bryan who watch 'Two Plus Two' and think I'm exactly like Katie Roberts in real life.''

"Watching you on TV is one thing, but living near you should make Bryan realize you are not Katie Roberts,'' he argued.

"We adults know that, but he's a little boy who's lost a parent. He's lonely and he wants life to be the way it was. I think it's only natural that he daydreams about having a mother,'' she said compassionately.

Impatience tightened his features. "Well, this is the real world, and wishful thinking is not going to change a thing, so I would appreciate you not encouraging such fantasies.''

That raised her hackles. "I'm not encouraging him to think of me as a possible stepmother!'' she protested indignantly. "First of all, I'm not looking to become anyone's mother, and second, I certainly don't need a husband.''

"No, I'm sure you don't.''

"And what is that supposed to mean?" she demanded hotly.

"It's obvious that you enjoy being single."

"Says whom?" When he didn't answer she added, "Oh, no, don't tell me you believe what you read in those tabloids?"

He made a sound of disgust. "No, I don't!"

"Good, because ninety percent of it is false."

"But you *are* single."

"That doesn't mean I don't want to get married and have children some day," she told him.

"Are you saying you just haven't met the right man?" Skepticism caused one eyebrow to lift.

"I haven't exactly been looking," she said coolly. "And despite what the tabloid papers say, I don't have chains of broken hearts strung throughout my apartment. Now if you'll excuse me, I'm tired and I'd like to go home."

She started to walk away, but he stopped her. "Alexis, wait. I'm sorry."

The apology came so unexpectedly it caught her totally off guard.

He shoved his hands into the pockets of his jeans. "Again, you did something nice for my son, and instead of being grateful I was out of line."

"Why is it so hard for you to believe that I care about Bryan?" she asked.

He held her gaze. "I know you care about him, Alexis. And he cares about you. That's why he arranged for you and me to be alone here at the beach.

He doesn't realize he's made it rather awkward for both of us.''

"He didn't intend for it to be embarrassing for either of us, I'm sure.'' She came to the ten-year-old's defense. "He probably thought you could use some quiet time to help you relax.''

Judd looked at the sun sinking over the water. "He's right about that. There never seems to be enough time for anything but work lately.'' Then, to her surprise, he looked her squarely in the eyes and asked, "Do you like pastrami on rye?''

"Are you inviting me to share your picnic?''

He nodded. "No strings attached, of course.''

Alexis was beginning to think it was impossible to do anything with the Shepards without there being strings. Still, she didn't want to refuse. "All right, I accept.''

"Good. I'll get the food.''

"There's probably a blanket in the trailer. Unless you brought one?''

He shook his head. "I figured we'd just sit at one of the tables.''

"Let me get a blanket, and I'll show you the perfect place for a quiet picnic.''

She led him to a narrow path through dense vegetation that opened onto a white expanse of sand. Alexis spread a red plaid blanket in a small area sheltered from the wind by large, craggy rocks.

"I'm surprised there aren't more people here,'' Judd remarked, glancing up and down the beach. He kicked off his shoes and socks, then rolled up the crisp hems of his trousers.

"Swimming's not good here." She kicked off her shoes and curled her toes into the sand. "But I like to come here, especially this time of day. It's a treat just to listen to the waves and gaze at the sun disappearing over the horizon." She spread her arms heavenward in an expression of sheer pleasure. "Most days it's dark by the time I leave the sound stage, and I miss all this."

"The ocean definitely has a calming effect, doesn't it?"

"Uh-huh," she agreed. "It looks like someone was working here earlier. Look. There's a sand castle" She pointed to a disintegrating pile of sand a short distance down the shore. "I'll race you to it."

Her slender legs churned, and she shot away from the startled Judd before he could get his footing. But thanks to much longer legs and an athletic strength, he matched his stride to hers.

"No fair," she panted as he overtook her. "I should have a head start."

"You *had* a head start."

Alexis was about to retort when she stumbled on a piece of driftwood. Judd's hand shot out to catch her, but the momentum of her fall brought them both down to the soft, grainy embrace of the sand, laughing and panting.

Alexis stretched out her arm and touched the disintegrating sand castle with her finger. "I won."

"Ha!" Judd's longer arm dug deeper into the wet pile. "*I* won!"

"I was first."

"But I went farthest." Judd lowered his face to hers until she could feel the warmth of his breath on her cheek. A wisp of her hair touched his jaw as it blew in the gentle breeze.

Neither of them moved. As the sun sank into the western sky and plunged below the vast space of gray water, they lay there, unable to stir, locked in a primeval battle of resistance and desire.

Alexis licked her lips nervously.

Judd's eyes darkened, and he leaned closer to her.

She didn't pull away. Instead she inhaled deeply, savoring the scent of him mixed with seawater and ocean air. She tasted the warm sweetness of his mouth and sank toward him, opening her lips to his until they were sharing a kiss so passionate it left her shuddering.

It was Judd who drew away. Alexis watched him spring to his feet, then offer her a hand. "I'm sorry, Alexis. That shouldn't have happened."

"Why not?" She allowed him to pull her to her feet, brushing sand from her clothing as she stood.

He didn't answer, but headed to where they had left the blanket. She walked beside him, wishing he hadn't withdrawn emotionally. For that's what he had done. Kissed her as if she were important to him, then shut her out as if she meant nothing.

They reached the blanket and he fell to his knees,

reaching for the sandwiches. "Two pastrami submarine sandwiches, potato chips and sodas." He set the food on the blanket. "I'm afraid it's rather simple fare for someone like you."

"I'm just an ordinary woman, Judd. I eat frozen dinners and fast food just like everyone else." She took a bite of her sandwich. "Mmm. Bryan doesn't know what he passed up."

"I hope he behaved himself at the taping this afternoon," Judd commented. "It was nice of you to invite him a second time."

"No problem. I knew we were filming on location and that it would be fun for him to bring Andy along."

Judd didn't comment, which made Alexis wonder if he thought it wasn't such a great idea. "I guess I was a little surprised that you allowed him to come."

"I'm slowly getting used to the idea that our neighbor is a television star."

"But it still bothers you, doesn't it?"

He took a sip of soda before answering. "I've discovered that celebrities are real people, too."

The look in his eyes had her heart racing. "Why, Judd, if I didn't know better I'd think you were paying me a compliment."

"I'm just being honest. I'm not the kind of man to play games, Alexis."

"I'm glad you're not. I work in an industry that has more than its share of players. Pretentiousness can be a way of life for many people in show business.

That's why I've always avoided socializing with the Hollywood crowd.''

"None of your friends are in the profession?''

"Some of them are, but my closest friends are those who knew me before I became Katie Roberts.'' She dabbed at her mouth with a napkin and took a sip of soda before continuing. "One thing about having celebrity status is that you often end up becoming rather suspicious of people's motives. You never know if people truly care about you or if they're just hanging around because of what you can do for them.''

"You're saying not everyone is up-front about what they want from you?''

She chuckled sarcastically. "Hardly. The public has a tendency to think that because I'm in the entertainment business they have a right to know everything about me.''

"I'm the public, and I don't know very much about you,'' he admitted.

"Do you want to know more about me?'' she asked boldly.

His dark eyes held hers. "Yes, I do. Maybe we should have dinner together.''

She held up her sandwich. "I thought that's what we were doing.''

"I mean a real dinner in a restaurant where you can choose your own entree,'' he answered with a grin.

Alexis found herself at a loss for words. When she

found her voice she asked, "Did you have a particular night in mind?"

"What about Saturday?"

"You don't have to work?" When he shook his head she asked, "What about Bryan? Can you get a sitter for him?"

"It shouldn't be a problem." A scowl creased his features. "Look, if you don't want to go, just say so."

"I want to have dinner with you. And Saturday would be fine."

He grinned—a wonderful smile that did funny things to Alexis's stomach. She thought how sad it was that he so seldom had occasion to smile.

"I can pick you up at eight."

"Eight would be good," she agreed.

When they had finished eating, they sat on a couple of boulders to drink in the beauty of the final stages of the setting sun. Out of the corner of her eye, Alexis noticed a couple of people slowly inching their way closer to them. She was experienced enough to know she had been recognized.

As she expected, it wasn't long before they approached her. She could see by the look on Judd's face that he didn't appreciate the interruption.

"Miss Gordon, I'm sorry to disturb you, but my son Joey is such a big fan of yours. Would it be a terrible imposition to ask you to autograph this for me?" The woman held up a scrap of paper and a pen.

Alexis fulfilled her request. She wrote a brief note

and signed the paper before handing it to the woman, hoping that it would be the end of it.

It wasn't. Next the woman whipped out a camera. "One picture...please?"

Alexis could see Judd withdrawing both physically and emotionally. She wanted to say no to the woman, but she knew if she said no, there was the chance the woman would snap a photo of her and Judd anyway.

"All right," she reluctantly agreed. She climbed from the boulder to pose with the woman while her husband snapped the picture.

Alexis was relieved when they left. She returned to the rock, but she sensed the easy camaraderie between them was gone.

"I guess this wasn't as quiet a place as I thought," she remarked.

When he didn't comment, she changed the subject. It wasn't long before he told her he needed to pick up Bryan. Alexis wondered if he was going to change his mind about the date and tell her it wasn't a good idea. He didn't, which she saw as a good sign. Maybe she had been foolish to think he would be scared away by a couple of autograph hounds.

Judd knew very little fear. The autograph seekers had reminded him how different his world was from the one where Alexis spent her time. She hadn't lied when she said the public thought her private life belonged not to her, but to everyone.

Judd had to decide whether or not he wanted to be

a part of that life. As much as he had enjoyed being with Alexis, he also knew he was a very private man. No matter where he took her to dinner on Saturday night they would undoubtedly be recognized by someone.

It was a dilemma he thought about as he drove home. He no longer doubted that Alexis was a genuine and sincere person. Nor did he have any uncertainty about his attraction to her. The better he got to know her, the more he liked her, which was what troubled him.

Was he being foolish to think about her as anything more than someone who wanted to have a good time? Just because she liked kissing him didn't mean she wanted to have a serious relationship with him. His body tensed at the memory of those kisses.

He never would have kissed her had it not been for Bryan. In fact, he probably wouldn't even know the woman were it not for his son. And this evening would have never happened had Bryan not orchestrated it.

With that thought, he pulled into the Kane driveway. When he went to the door, Andy's mother greeted him with a grim face.

"Oh, Mr. Shepard. I'm glad you're here. Bryan's not feeling well," she said as she ushered him inside.

"What seems to be the problem?" Judd asked.

"His stomach is upset." She led him into a bedroom, where Bryan lay huddled on the bed. "I gave him something soothing to drink, but I don't think it helped.''

Judd approached the bed with suspicion on his mind. Was this his son's way of avoiding chastisement for playing matchmaker? "Bryan?"

Several groans preceded a weak answer. "Hi, Dad.''

"Are you going to be okay?"

"I think so," he said weakly. "I think I'd better lay down in the back seat."

Judd nodded and helped his son out to the car. Once he was settled, Judd hopped into the driver's seat and started up the engine. He was tempted to let his son have a scolding, but he wasn't sure if Bryan's misery was an act.

Once they were home, Judd helped him get into his pajamas and climb into bed. Any doubt that the ten-year-old was feigning illness was erased when Judd touched his forehead.

"You're hot. You really don't feel good, do you?"

"Uh-uh. Dad, you're not mad that I went home with Andy, are you?"

Judd would have liked to lecture his son about tricking people into doing things they didn't want to do, but he found he couldn't. Bryan was sick, and Judd wasn't unhappy at the way the evening had turned out.

Judd smoothed the hair from Bryan's brow. "I'm not mad, son. Now you need to get some sleep, and we'll talk in the morning, okay?"

"Okay."

Before Judd turned out the light, Bryan had one more question. "Dad, Alexis wasn't mad at me, was she?"

"No," he answered honestly.

"Good. Cuz I really like her and I don't want her to be mad at me ever."

"Neither do I." Judd pulled the door shut, then repeated, "Neither do I."

CHAPTER EIGHT

THE word *uncomfortable* didn't even come close to describing Judd's feelings as he showered and shaved for his date with Alexis. And it didn't help one bit that Bryan was taking in the entire process with endless fascination and glee.

"Where are you taking her, Dad? Someplace nice? Maybe she'd like the Weenie Roaster or Chuck's Chick Inn. They're both really good." Bryan swung his legs from his perch on the closed toilet and practically salivated at the idea.

"I have a hunch she might like something a little more…exotic," Judd said, suppressing a smile. "There's a new Greek restaurant that's just opened, and it's supposed to be wonderful. I have reservations there. Mrs. Wahlstrom has the phone number in case of an emergency."

"Greek? Yuck. You'll never catch a woman that way, Dad."

Judd raised an eyebrow in surprise. "Catch a woman? Is that what you think I'm trying to do? And where did you pick up that phrase?"

"Andy told me. He said if you asked Katie, I mean Alexis out on a date, you must have the hots for her and you're trying to catch her."

"Remind me to prohibit you from spending so much time with Andy," Judd said wryly. "The boy is entirely too sophisticated, as well as badly informed."

"You do like Alexis though, right?" The hope in Bryan's voice was almost painful to hear.

"Yes, but that doesn't mean…" He searched for the right words to describe his relationship with Alexis. "This is an opportunity for me to get to know her better, that's all. We're friends—just like you and Andy." Judd debated between the white shirt and the pale blue, wishing Bryan would find someone else to torment with his questions.

"Aren't you gonna kiss her?"

"Bryan, that's enough. Go get the navy jacket lying on my bed."

"Your new jacket? You are going to kiss her!" Bryan gave a whoop and jumped off the toilet seat.

Judd closed his eyes and counted to ten.

After numerous unwelcome compliments from both Bryan and Mrs. Wahlstrom, Judd escaped into the hall, reminding the pair that they were not to open the door or try to eavesdrop while he was escorting Alexis to the car.

When he rang Alexis's doorbell, she called, "It's open. Come in."

She was still barefoot, and struggling with the clasp of her gold necklace. "Almost ready. Could you help me with this?" She turned her back to him with an end of the chain in each hand. Her dress was zipped only halfway up her back, exposing creamy skin that smelled like apricots. "I've never been able to work well when I can't see what I'm doing."

Judd willed his hands not to tremble as he hooked the clasp. It wasn't as if he'd never clasped a necklace or seen bare skin before. But it had been a long time. Too long.

"The zipper, too, if you don't mind. I think it's stuck."

Silently Judd worked the zipper free, trying to steady fingers tempted by warm, soft flesh. Finally the lush expanse of back was covered, and he quickly jammed his hands in his pockets. "There. All done."

Completely unaware of his reaction to her, Alexis meandered toward her kitchen. "I've chilled some wine. Do we have time before our dinner reservations?"

He glanced at his watch, wishing the hour were later. "Yes." He wasn't sure how long he wanted to stay alone with her in this apartment. Here was a woman he mistrusted because of her profession and objected to because of his son's infatuation with her, and yet every pulse point in his body was throbbing.

"It's my favorite Chardonnay." Alexis handed him a crystal glass with a delicate stem. Still barefoot, she melted into the opposite end of the couch on which Judd had taken a seat and curled her feet under her. Her knees were touching his thigh.

Judd threw back a swallow so quickly he thought he might choke.

"Are you all right?" she asked with concern.

"Fine." He cleared his throat, then held up his glass saying, "This is good, but I think we'd better go. We don't want to be late if traffic is heavy."

She looked disappointed. "It's a waste of a good wine. It shouldn't be hurried."

Judd agreed, but the longer he sat beside Alexis, the more difficult it was to keep his hands off her. And he was certain that if he did touch her, dinner might not happen. She was more tantalizing than he had ever imagined she could be, and it was with a supreme effort that he finally led her from the apartment.

Traffic was light, and they arrived at the restaurant early. Fortunately, there was a table ready for them. Judd ordered a stiff drink for himself and a Chardonnay for Alexis.

"What would you like?" he asked.

"I haven't been here before. Why don't you order and surprise me?" She swirled the wine in her glass.

"Are you sure?"

"Order away."

He asked for tzatziki and calamari for appetizers, stuffed grape leaves, moussaka and then a sampler plate of pastries, including baklava, for dessert.

"You do know the camera adds ten pounds, don't you? This meal could add another ten!" Alexis told him when the waiter had departed.

"You don't look any different on TV than you do

in person,'' Judd said gallantly, then almost bit his lip for letting that bit of information slip out.

"So you do watch the show?" Alexis sounded delighted.

"Ah, it's hard to miss when Bryan is glued to the set. It's his most important half hour of the week."

"That's very flattering to me," she said, her smile powerful enough to light up the entire room. No wonder it was burning his insides.

"Yes, but I'm afraid it's not so good for Bryan," he said soberly.

"You're worried that he's fantasizing about a mother, aren't you." There was a compassion in her voice Judd knew was genuine.

"He's got to accept where we are as a family now," Judd insisted. "There are just the two of us, and no amount of wishing or fantasizing is going to change that."

"It's only natural that he misses his mother."

"Missing her is one thing, trying to replace her is another." He took a sip of his drink and lowered his eyes before she could see the pain in them. He hadn't been quick enough.

Her hand reached out to cover his. "Your wife must have been a wonderful person to have been loved so much by both of you."

Judd felt the familiar pain of loss. He tried not to think of Carol often, hoping the wound would heal if he didn't pay it any attention. Besides, he was not one to wallow in self-pity.

Normally he would have changed the subject, but with Alexis it was different. He found himself saying, "Carol was a lovely person, a great mother. Couldn't have been better, in fact. She and Bryan spent many hours together every day."

"Poor little guy," Alexis said, "no wonder he's lonesome. He lost not only his mother but probably his best friend, as well."

Judd stared over her head at a framed poster depicting the Aegean Sea. "I never thought about it that way before, but I suppose it's true."

When he would have stopped talking about her, Alexis urged him to continue.

"She was very playful and fun-loving. Sometimes I'd come home from a call exhausted and find her and Bryan having a picnic on the front lawn. There would be a beach umbrella, blankets, a boom box, balloons, and they'd be eating whatever Bryan had picked out—peanut butter and jelly sandwiches, chips and salsa, those horrible store-bought cookies kids love— and always big mugs of milk. Carol never let a meal go by without milk."

His smile was bittersweet. "She was a calcium freak. Said she didn't want to grow old and be all stooped over with osteoporosis." Bitter laughter choked his throat. "No danger of that, as it turned out."

"I am so sorry," Alexis said, giving his hand a gentle squeeze.

Her touch was warm, her eyes compassionate. Just

when he would have raised her hand to his lips, the waiter arrived with their appetizers. The connection between them had been broken.

"The calamari looks good," Alexis said in a husky voice.

By candlelight she was more beautiful than ever. Judd found himself sliding closer to her, wanting to feel her warmth, to inhale the fragrance he was coming to recognize as hers alone.

"Have you had tzatziki before?" He dipped a crust of bread into a bowl of pasty-looking stuff with flecks of cucumber in it.

She followed his lead. "Mmm, it's good! But it looks so bland." Then she began to giggle. "Speaking of bland, you should have heard the twins on the set the other day. They were supposed to be eating ice cream for a scene and, of course, since ice cream melts so quickly, the prop department had given them cold mashed potatoes with chocolate sauce and cherries. The faces they made! You'd have thought they were being poisoned. Of course, I suppose they were expecting real ice cream, so the first bite was a bit of a shock."

"You're ruining the fantasy," Judd teased. "Now I'll never believe ice cream is really ice cream on television again."

"The boys were troupers, though. Next take, they behaved as if it was the most wonderful-tasting stuff in the world. They are good little actors."

"You enjoy it, don't you? Television and acting, I

mean." Judd thoughtfully picked at the calamari on his plate.

"Acting, yes. Television…well, let's just say it's a living."

Judd was surprised at the indifference in her voice. "A living?"

"The hours are too long, the schedule is crazy, and it's hard work," she explained.

"And here I thought you had it made."

"I'm doing very well—don't get me wrong. It's just that I've always dreamed of being on the big screen—you know, doing feature-length films."

"Is that going to happen somewhere in the future?"

"I hope so." She took another bite of tzatziki, then grinned sheepishly. "You can be sure that if there's any way I can make it happen, I will."

"I would imagine films are more lucrative," Judd said uneasily, not wanting to think she was materialistic.

"You've seen the salaries the big stars are getting." She shook her head in amazement. "Yes, the money would be nice, but that's not why I want it, not completely."

That surprised him. "Then why?"

"Truthfully?" When he nodded she said, "I'm homesick."

The stuffed grape leaves and moussaka arrived, and Judd had to restrain himself from asking more questions. *Homesick?* What did that have to do with anything?

When they were alone again, drinks refreshed and plates of delicious smelling, steaming food in front of them, Judd asked, "What do you mean about being homesick?"

"Contrary to what the tabloids would have people believe, I do have a family that I'm very close to. I didn't just rise up out of some plastic surgeon's office. And before you even think anywhere along that line, no, I have not had anything on my body surgically altered."

"Then nature was very good to you," he said with an admiring glance at her figure.

To his surprise, she blushed. "Thank you."

"So tell me about this family you miss."

"Well, I'm the oldest of four kids. I have two sisters and a brother. I practically raised them and sometimes I get so lonely for them, I could cry. My phone bills would put the national debt to shame. One of my sisters has two babies already, and I never get to spend time with them. I'm afraid they won't even know their auntie Alexis. And my younger sister recently got engaged, so there's a wedding to plan."

"The reason you're making the quilt."

She nodded. "Luckily the wedding's taking place during the hiatus of 'Two Plus Two.' That's what's nice about films. I could live in Colorado near my family and travel to location for the time I'd be needed. At least then I'd get to be a part of their lives some of the time.''

Judd was pleasantly surprised by her words.

"I do love acting and wouldn't do anything else,'' she continued. "I'm known in the business for being focused and willing to take risks to get where I want to be.''

"Ruthless,'' Judd quoted one of the tabloids his secretary had shown him.

"That, too. I just don't usually tell anyone why I'm so ruthless. You can't be soft in Hollywood or you'll get stepped over by everyone wanting your spot. Directors and producers aren't sure you're committed, agents think you'll run out on them, aspiring actresses vie for your place. It's a tough business, Judd, and I've had to become tough or I wouldn't have survived.''

Then she grinned. "Of course, I was no softie when I came. My sisters and brother are a rowdy bunch. I've crawled into bed many a night to a short-sheeted bed. Not to mention salt in the sugar bowl, trick water glasses that leaked or flies frozen into my ice cubes.''

He raised his eyebrows. "And you want to spend time with these people?''

Alexis laughed. "They are also the ones who supported my decision to become an actress and believed in me when I was living on beans and rice in a cheap efficiency apartment trying to get an audition. We're good together, and they are family. What else can I say?''

They were barely done with their meal when the pastries arrived with strong cups of Greek coffee. The rest of their conversation was light and flirtatious.

At the apartment complex, Alexis kicked off her shoes as they crossed the soft hallway carpet. Judd didn't want to see the evening end, yet he knew Mrs. Wahlstrom had to get home.

As they stood face to face outside her door, it seemed natural to end the evening with a kiss. Judd lifted her chin with his finger, intending to lightly brush her lips with his. Only once his mouth met hers, there was no stopping the emotions that had them clinging to each other. What started as a tender kiss became a sensuous exploration that left both of them breathless and craving more.

Reluctantly, Judd released her. "I'd like to see you again, Alexis."

"I'd like that, too," she said softly.

Neither one noticed that Bryan had slipped out of bed and cracked the front door of the apartment to watch for their return. By the time Judd turned the key in his door, the ten-year-old had scooted back to bed.

"What's with you today, son?" Judd asked over breakfast.

Bryan was shoveling cereal into his mouth as though he were taking part in a race. He'd already spilled his juice and practically swallowed a slice of toast whole.

"Gotta hurry. I need to talk to Andy. May I be excused?"

"All right." He set his napkin aside. "I might as well leave, too."

They walked together to the corner, where Andy was already waiting for the school bus. Judd waited with him until the bus arrived.

"Wait till I tell you my news!" Bryan blurted the moment they'd found a seat at the back of the bus. "I think I'm getting a new mom!"

"No kidding? Who?"

"Katie...I mean Alexis. She and my dad went on a date last night, and when they came home I saw them kissing."

"Gross!"

"I know, but adults seem to like it. I could tell my dad did." Bryan sat back in the hard leather seat with a blissful smile on his face. "She's gonna be a great mom."

He and Andy had no more opportunity to discuss Bryan's big news until they were at Bryan's apartment after school. Mrs. Wahlstrom was busy washing and ironing clothes to a fifties station. Buddy Holly was turned up loud and she was singing as she worked.

It was the perfect time for a private discussion.

"So did you really see her kiss him? Like on the lips?" Andy asked lasciviously.

"Right on. Then she wiped away some lipstick from his lip." Bryan shuddered. "I would have thrown up if a girl did that to me, but when Dad turned around he was grinning.''

"Weird," Andy concluded. "So when do you think they'll get married?"

"I don't know. Soon, I hope. Don't kisses mean things are pretty serious between people?"

Judd, who had come home early for once, stood frozen in the doorway. *Kisses? Married? Just exactly what does Bryan know—or think he knows—about last night?*

He backed into the hallway and made a second, considerably more noisy entrance. Bryan and Andy looked up guiltily.

"Hi, boys." Judd made his voice light and saw the pair relax immediately.

Andy, no dummy, jumped off the couch and announced, "I'd better go."

He was out of the apartment before Judd could even say goodbye, leaving Judd to wonder what had been said *before* he'd arrived.

"Bryan? What were you boys taking about?" Judd sat on the couch next to his son and pulled him close for as much of a hug as Bryan would allow.

"Just stuff."

"What kind of stuff?"

Bryan began to blush until he was red to the roots of his hair. "You'll be mad if I tell you."

"Then I'll also probably be mad if you don't."

Bryan reluctantly said, "I saw you and Alexis kissing last night."

"So you were up pretty late."

"I went right back to bed. I just wanted to know if you had fun." He gave a boyish grin. "And it looked like you did. Dad, is Alexis going to be my new mom?"

"Bryan! Just because a man and woman kiss doesn't mean they're going to get married. Sometimes people kiss just as a way of saying thank-you or good-night."

"That's all?" Bryan sounded disappointed.

"Yes. That is all."

Tears of disappointment filled Bryan's eyes. "But I thought…"

Judd could see how easy it would be for his son to jump to conclusions. Bryan wanted Alexis to be the mother she played on TV. Judd wondered if he was making a mistake seeing her again.

"Alexis and I had dinner, Bryan, as friends," he explained calmly. "Now that your mother's gone, there could be other women I take to dinner. It's what single men do—they date." He frowned. "Now go tell Mrs. Wahlstrom that she can go home for the day," he instructed. Then he went into the kitchen to fix himself a drink. That little conversation had confirmed what Judd already knew—when it came to a relationship with a woman, he needed to consider Bryan's feelings.

The fact that he was thinking about a relationship with a woman other than Carol told Judd something important had changed in his life. Some of the ice around his heart had melted, and it felt good.

The only problem was the uncertainty he faced regarding Alexis. What if he were wrong about her and the tabloids were right? She could be a heartbreaker—happy to be a part of his and Bryan's lives today yet able to say goodbye to them tomorrow without a shred of regret.

Of one thing he was sure. His son had already given his heart to their lovely neighbor, and he was in danger of losing his, too.

When Bryan asked if he could sleep over at Andy's the following night, Judd saw it as the perfect opportunity for him to follow his own instincts. And right now his instincts were telling him to see Alexis.

When she opened the door and smiled at him, he knew he had made the right decision. She wore pale yellow sweats with matching shoes and white socks sporting a yellow flower on each ankle. Her lush hair was pulled casually from her face with a pale grosgrain ribbon. She didn't look like anyone's mother this evening, but more like a teenager, her face scrubbed free of makeup.

"What's up?" Alexis asked.

"I want to take you somewhere. Are you free?"

"Right now?"

"Yeah." He held his breath, waiting for her answer.

"Sure," she answered, and he felt a great weight

being lifted from his chest. "Do I get to know where this somewhere is?"

"It'll be more fun if you don't," he answered, fighting the urge to take her in his arms and kiss her senseless.

She shrugged and grinned. "Okay. I'm all yours. Let me put Iggy in his cage, and I'll be ready."

"Heights don't bother you, do they?" he asked as she locked her door.

"This is getting more exciting by the minute," she said in delight. "And no, I don't have a problem with heights."

"Great." He escorted her to the Jeep where they climbed inside.

Along the way she quizzed him relentlessly, trying to guess what his surprise could be. It was only as they pulled through the gates at the small airstrip that she had a clue as to their destination.

"Is this where you work?"

"We're in that brick building ahead—the one with the narrow windows and bright green awnings," he replied. "You can see by the number of hangars we're not the only flying service that uses this airstrip."

He drove along the service road to the building. "We're going to go up in that chopper over there."

"Don't you have to keep it free for emergencies?"

"It's not part of our fleet yet, but I want to put a few hours on it to see how I like it. I hope you like flying."

"Oh, I do! I remember getting a helicopter ride as

a kid and I loved it.'' Her eyes sparkled at the memory. ''I always thought helicopters looked like bugs— big, fat, funny bugs.''

Judd laughed. ''That's the first time I've ever heard that particular description. Come inside and meet some of the employees.''

''They're still here? This late?''

''Someone is here day and night. Emergencies usually don't happen at convenient times.'' He led her to a large but cozy lounge. Two men were stretched out on couches watching television.

''Hi, boss, what's up?'' The younger of the two swung his feet to the floor while the other man waved from his comfortable position.

''No calls?''

''Not yet. I hope it's a quiet night.''

Judd turned to Alexis. ''We have pilots here and on call twenty-four hours a day. They can be in their choppers and on their way in less than five minutes. We do rescues, hospital transfers, whatever.'' He turned to the pilots. ''I'm going to take Alexis for a ride.''

''Are you Alexis Gordon, the television star?''

''That's me,'' she said cheerfully.

''My kids watch your show all the time.''

After a few minutes of small talk, Judd ushered her outside and into the helicopter. It was a still and beautiful night, perfect for flying. He buckled Alexis into her seat and made the necessary checks and procedures before liftoff. Then, light and graceful as one of those bugs Alexis had mentioned, they were in the sky, tilting to the passenger side so that Alexis could get a full view of the city.

"This is spectacular!" she gasped. "Absolutely the most beautiful thing I've ever seen. I always like to fly in at night to see the lights, but in this I feel so much closer to them. It's as though I could reach out and touch some of them."

"Is there anything special you'd like to see?"

"Everything," Alexis breathed, spellbound.

"That could take a while," Judd commented. "First I'll take you downtown and then to the shoreline."

"I have all night," Alexis said. "And I'd love to spend it like this."

"I thought you'd be out on some exotic date—a film premiere or something."

"To be photographed and pushed about by the crowds? No, thank you. I'd rather walk a lizard."

He knew that to be true. Enjoying her enjoyment, Judd flew over the studio and their apartment building, then down to Anaheim to see the theme park. Finally, he returned to the airstrip.

When he opened her door, Alexis nearly fell into his arms. "That was the most wonderful ride of my life! Thank you."

He could smell the soft fragrance of her shampoo and the headier scent of perfume as she hugged him tight. He closed his eyes and inhaled deeply.

"You are like no man I've ever met," Alexis stated frankly. "You have access to the stars!"

He didn't even comment on her unintentional pun, but led her to the building. Both pilots had disappeared.

"Where did your men go?"

"To bed. The best night's work in this place is getting a full night's sleep. Let's go see if they left any food in the kitchen."

The kitchen was compact but efficient. And there were two bowls of chili covered in clear wrap waiting to be heated in the microwave.

While the chili warmed, Judd made hot chocolate and found half a loaf of French bread. When he served the food, Alexis dug in as though she hadn't eaten in a week.

As she scraped the bottom of the bowl, she noticed Judd staring at her. "What's wrong?"

"Nothing. You are perfectly normal. I just expected a woman in your business…with a figure like yours…well, not to eat so much."

"I'm a country girl at heart—and stomach. Besides, I was blessed with a great metabolism and a lot of energy for exercising. That's why I swim in the pool nearly every day. Bryan likes to race me."

When he frowned she said, "It's good for both of us. I usually win, but Bryan's skill and strength are growing quickly. He'll be beating me any day now."

"I didn't realize you spent so much time with him," Judd admitted reluctantly.

"Well, he does appear quite often to play with Iggy. Sometimes we play a few games before he leaves, or watch television. Bryan is a neat kid. You've done a good job with him. I have to admit, I've grown very fond of him."

"I don't need to tell you the feeling is mutual." He eyed her pensively. "I have to take back something I said previously. You *are* the motherly type."

"I've had plenty of experience. If there was one thing I learned it was that kids like structure and discipline even though they're cheering for anarchy and chaos most of the time."

Judd agreed with her. The better he got to know Alexis, the more he realized she was not only sincere, but bright and introspective. She seemed almost too good to be true.

He thought about the articles in the tabloids. Even if they were false, he couldn't help but wonder what role he would play in her life. Man number twenty? Thirty? More?

Judd was so out of touch with the Hollywood lifestyle he had no idea what to expect. Alexis seemed different, special. Her joy at the helicopter ride was genuine. She'd relished the simple food he'd served and told him how much she cared about his son. Could it all be an act?

"Is everything okay?" she asked. He realized he had been lost in his thoughts.

One look in her eyes had him replying, "Everything's great."

"Good, because I like being with you, Judd."

She gave him that smile that set every nerve ending in his body tingling with pleasure. It also warned him that getting involved with Alexis could bring heartbreak or happiness.

It didn't matter. It was too late for any warnings. She already had a place in his heart.

CHAPTER NINE

"DAD! Dad! Look! I'm in the paper!" Bryan came rushing through the door waving a newspaper in his hand. He shoved it under Judd's nose. "When Alexis took me to the zoo we got our picture taken and they put it in the paper!"

Judd felt a knot in his stomach as he looked at the photograph of his son sitting next to the television star. It looked so natural, the two of them side by side on a park bench, peering at the guidebook. The caption beneath the photo said, Alexis Gordon Plays Mom Off the Set.

"Ain't it cool, Dad?"

"Isn't," Judd automatically corrected, his eyes scanning the page for a story. There was none, just a short column that said Alexis had been seen spending a lot of time with a motherless boy. No mention was made of Bryan's name, to Judd's relief. The last line of the article was, "Who says life doesn't imitate art?"

"Have you shown this to Alexis?" Judd asked.

"Uh-uh. She's still at work." Impatient to have the paper in his hands, Bryan gently tugged on it until his dad released it. "This is so cool! Everyone in school

150

is going to know that Alexis is..." He trailed off a bit sheepishly.

"Is what?" Judd asked when he didn't finish.

"My friend?"

Judd's eyes pinned his son. "That *is* all you've said about Alexis, isn't it?"

He nodded vigorously, but Judd wasn't convinced. "Bryan, you haven't told the kids at school that Alexis is going to be your mother, have you?"

"Just Andy. And I did like you told me. I told him that just because you're dating doesn't mean you're going to get married."

"We're not exactly dating," Judd protested. "We're just spending some time together getting to know one another."

"You mean she's not your girlfriend? Then how come you always put all that good-smelling stuff on when you go over to see her?"

Judd changed the subject as he headed into the kitchen. "Tell me what happened at school today."

"It was boring," Bryan answered. "Can we call Grandpa and Grandma and tell them my picture's in the paper?"

"Maybe after dinner. Go wash up. Mrs. Wahlstrom left a big bowl of taco salad for us in the refrigerator. We need to eat dinner so you can get to your baseball practice."

"I know. I'm going to take the paper so I can show the rest of the guys," he boasted.

"Am I supposed to be at this practice with you?" Judd asked.

"Uh-uh. Andy's mom said if you drop us off, she'll pick us up."

"Sounds like a good plan," Judd answered.

So after dinner Judd drove the two boys, with bats and gloves in hand, to the athletic field at school. When he returned home, he noticed the red convertible in the garage. On an impulse, he walked past his door to Alexis's and knocked.

To his surprise a man answered. He wore a black silk shirt open at the neck where a thick gold chain hugged his throat. Rings graced several fingers on a hand that held a cocktail glass filled with amber liquid.

"Is Alexis around?" Judd asked, trying not to be intimidated by the man's curious appraisal.

"She can't come to the door right now. Is there something I can help you with?" The clipped tones held a hint of hostility.

Uneasiness flowed through Judd's veins like water. "I'm Judd Shepard. I live across the hall."

The hostility slid away, and a grin spread cheeks tanned by hours in the sun. "Oh—Bryan's father! Come on in. I'm Ray Conway, Alexis's publicist." He stood with the door open, waiting for Judd to enter, as if he were the keeper of Alexis's home.

It didn't make Judd happy. Nor did the fact that this man knew his son.

Judd took a step backward. "Er, it's all right. I can talk to Alexis another time."

Ray stretched a hand out invitingly. "Don't be silly. Come on in and have a drink. She's in the shower but she'll be out in a couple of minutes."

In the shower? Uneasiness echoed through Judd. "No, just tell Alexis I was here."

The agent shrugged. "Whatever."

Judd went to his apartment, where he restlessly prowled, wondering what Alexis's relationship was to the man. Why would she allow him free reign of her apartment while she took a shower? All sorts of unsettling images flashed in his mind. He quickly pushed them aside, along with the jealousy that had bounced around his gut ever since the man had answered her door.

He needed to remember that Ray Conway was her publicist, not her lover. There was no need to have such a reaction to the situation. On an impulse, Judd got in his car and drove to the florist. He bought a simple yet beautiful bouquet of daffodils and daisies. He would give them to Alexis after her guest had gone home.

He drove to the apartment complex and parked his car. As he walked around the garage he heard two voices. One he recognized as belonging to Alexis, the other to her publicist.

"Thank goodness for Bryan Shepard," the man said in obvious glee.

The mention of his son's name stopped Judd cold. He stayed behind a hedge, listening to them.

"He's a sweet kid." Judd heard Alexis say.

"He's going to help you get that role you wanted."

"I can't believe one photograph can sway a studio."

"Believe it, baby. Everyone knows you play a terrific mom on television. What they don't know is what you do in real life. That's why I wanted you to get photographed with that kid. In this business, image is everything. You know that. Now everyone thinks you've taken him under your wing and that you really are as maternal as Katie Roberts."

What Alexis's response was, Judd didn't know, for they passed out of hearing range. Two car doors slammed. As Judd stepped around the building, he saw a silver Jag disappearing down the drive.

So Alexis's interest in Bryan had been for publicity purposes. If Judd hadn't heard the words himself he wouldn't have believed it. The appearances at school, the visits to her apartment, the birthday party...all had been for one reason only. To further her career.

It was with a bitter taste in his mouth that Judd headed to his apartment. As he passed the trash receptacle, he dropped the bouquet of flowers inside.

Alexis had not seen Judd all week. She figured it was because they both were working long hours and at different times of the day. However, when the weekend came and went without her seeing either of the

Shepards, she began to suspect that Judd might be avoiding her.

She didn't understand why, unless he was worried that Bryan was getting too attached to her. Alexis knew it was a concern for Judd, and she understood. She hadn't wanted to fall in love with Judd Shepard, yet that was exactly what had happened. When or how she wasn't sure. All she knew was that the Shepard boys had found a way into her heart, and she didn't want them to vacate that place.

That's why, when she arrived home early on Monday, she waited for Bryan to return from school. When she saw the bus, she grabbed her in-line skates and headed outdoors.

"Hi, Alexis," he called, his backpack slung over his shoulder.

"Hey, Bryan. What's up?"

"For once I don't have any homework," he declared jubilantly. "That means I can play outside before dinner."

"I was just thinking about going skating. Want to join me?" she asked.

"Sure! I have to tell Mrs. Wahlstrom and get my skates." He disappeared inside and returned a few minutes later sporting knee pads and carrying his skates. "Where are we going?"

She fished a set of keys from her jeans pocket. "I thought we'd go to that park over on Canyon Drive. You know, the one with the new bandshell."

"Cool! Andy says you can skate all the way down to the ocean from there."

"That's what I hear." She opened the trunk and gestured for him to place his skates inside.

While they drove to the park she asked him about school and baseball, avoiding any mention of his father. It was Bryan who brought up the subject.

"You and my dad didn't have a fight or anything, did you?" he asked.

"No, why do you ask?"

He shrugged. "When I asked him if you could come over and have pizza with us yesterday he said he didn't think it was a good idea and when I asked why not he just got this crabby look on his face and told me the discussion was over."

"Maybe your father was tired. He works very hard."

"Yeah, he does," he said with a sigh of resignation.

Alexis thought it best if she change the subject. "Tell me when your first baseball game is going to be played. I'd like to come."

"Really?"

"Sure. I watch my brother play when I can get home. I was also on my school's softball team," she told him. "I played third base."

"It'll probably be when you're at work," Bryan warned her.

"Not if it's after next week. That's when the taping of the last episode of 'Two Plus Two' takes place."

"Does that mean you'll be on vacation?"

"For a while. I'm going to Colorado to visit my family. Then I have to do some other things, like personal appearances, commercials and guest spots on some of the talk shows."

"It must be so much fun," he said dreamily.

"It's tiring."

"You don't like to do all that stuff?"

"It's all right, but I'd rather be skating." She pulled into the recreation area and parked. "Are you ready?"

He nodded eagerly and climbed out of the Mercedes. With youthful abandon, he laced up his skates and adjusted his knee pads.

"Don't you have any wrist guards?" Alexis asked when he stood poised, ready to roll.

"Forgot them. Besides, Andy says they're for sissies."

She pulled a pair out of her pocket, and he grinned sheepishly. "You're a girl. You can wear them." She gave him a dubious look and he added, "You don't need to worry. I never fall."

"I'm not so sure it's a good idea for you to skate without them."

"It's all right. Honest. Lots of times my dad lets me go without them. Besides, my knees are the things that usually get scraped up."

Alexis pushed aside her apprehension and started out along the paved trail. She soon discovered that Bryan wasn't quite as skilled on the skates as he wanted her to believe. Despite his attempts at difficult maneuvers, he was unable to convince her he was ready to give anyone lessons. As they coasted down a sharp decline, he tried to show off for the umpteenth time.

"Bryan, I really wish you wouldn't try to do tricks. Please be careful." Her words of warning came too late.

He spun out of control and went crashing to the pavement. Panic rose in Alexis's throat as she saw him sprawled on the ground.

"Are you all right?" she asked, stooping beside him.

As hard as he tried not to cry, tears trickled down his cheeks. The knee pads had protected him from any serious scrapes, but there were still abrasions on his legs, and the fall had caused an injury to his left arm.

"It hurts really bad," he cried, propping up the injured forearm with his right hand.

As Alexis took a closer look, she noticed it wasn't his arm, but his wrist that was injured. Medical attention was definitely needed. She helped Bryan to his feet, then escorted him to the car, being careful to make sure he didn't lose his balance and fall again.

At the car, she unlaced his skates and helped him into his shoes. Then she drove to the nearest clinic. On the way she phoned Lifeline Flying Service, only to learn that Judd was on a flight.

By the time he received the message that Bryan had fallen and had been taken to a clinic, the doctor had already determined that the injury was a broken wrist. When Judd arrived, Bryan sat with his left arm encased in plaster.

"How does it feel?" he asked his son, concern softening the hard angles of his handsome face.

"Sore," Bryan answered.

"How did this happen?" He directed the question to Alexis.

"We were skating, and he fell."

"He was with you?"

She nodded. "At that park on Canyon Drive."

"The one with all the hills?" There was a look of disbelief in his eyes. "That's not exactly beginner territory."

Bryan piped up. "I wouldn't have fallen, Dad, if I hadn't been trying to show Alexis how to do a turn going downhill."

Judd looked dubious.

"I tried to warn him, but..." Alexis trailed off. She sounded lame even to her ears.

Judd surveyed the cast on his son's arm. "Must have been a pretty hard fall if you broke a bone wearing the wrist guards."

Bryan and Alexis exchanged glances. "I didn't have them on," Bryan confessed weakly.

Judd turned to Alexis. "You didn't make sure that he was properly protected?"

"I'm sorry. He forgot to bring them along and he told me you let him skate without them all the time."

Alexis defended herself, although she knew Judd had a point. She shouldn't have let Bryan skate without the protective guards.

"Sometimes you don't make me wear them," Bryan reminded his father.

Judd raked a hand through his hair, then without another word went to talk to the doctor. When he returned, the creases were gone from his forehead, but his disposition hadn't improved.

As they left the clinic, Bryan asked his father if he could ride home with Alexis. Judd scowled and said, "You'll ride home with me."

Unhappy with his father's answer, Bryan twisted out of Judd's grasp, his lower lip pushed out in defiance. Alexis could see that he was going to protest.

"It's probably better if you go with your father, Bryan. I have to make a couple of stops on the way home," she said gently.

"But my skates are in your car."

"You can get them later," Judd stated firmly.

Bryan's shoulders slumped in resignation.

"How about if I bring them over after dinner?" Alexis suggested brightly.

"That won't be necessary," Judd answered. "Just leave them in the hallway, and one of us will pick them up."

Alexis felt as if she'd been firmly put in her place. *Just leave them in the hallway?* If she had any doubt in her mind that he was angry with her, it was gone now. There had not been even a hint of warmth in his voice.

She placed her hand on his forearm. "I'm really sorry this happened, Judd."

"This all could have been avoided—" He stopped abruptly. So engrossed were they in the emotional war going on between them that neither had noticed the photographer across the street. It was Bryan who saw the man taking pictures.

"Why is that guy taking pictures of us?"

Judd glared at the man behind the zoom lens. "You'd better ask Alexis that question." He whisked Bryan into the Jeep, leaving a frustrated Alexis staring after them.

One of the stops Alexis made on the way home was at DJ's, where she purchased a caramel-topped ice cream pizza with peanuts and hot fudge sauce. If Judd thought she was going to dump Bryan's skates outside his door and disappear, he was mistaken.

Later that evening, with Bryan's skates slung over her arm and the pizza in her hands, she rang the Shepards' doorbell. As she expected, Judd answered. Her heart started to race.

"Hi. I brought Bryan's skates back." She gave him a genuine smile. She wanted to convey to him how happy she was to see him.

It had no effect on him. He didn't show any emotion. He simply took the skates from her and said, "Thank you."

She held up the box containing the ice cream pizza. "I also brought him something to ease the pain."

He looked as if he wanted to shut the door in her face. He didn't. "Bryan's asleep. It must have been the painkillers they gave him, but he conked out right after dinner."

"Oh." She took a deep breath and said, "Luckily this will keep until tomorrow. Do you want me to take it, or should I put it in your freezer?" She looked over his shoulder, hoping he would invite her inside.

Indecision had his mouth twisting until finally he said, "I'll take it."

He took the box from her hands and again looked as if he wanted to close the door on her. She could hardly believe this was the same man who only last week had taken her on a romantic flight across the city.

"I'd better put this in the refrigerator before it melts." His tone was blunt as well as dismissive.

Alexis had had enough of his indifference. She looked him squarely in the eye and said, "You don't need to worry. There's no chance of that happening as long as you're holding it."

"You think I'm cold?"

"Yes," she said boldly. "Look, I've apologized for not insisting Bryan wear his wrist guards. I made an error in judgment, and if I could go back and do things differently, I would. I didn't want to see Bryan get hurt."

"No, I don't suppose you did. Not when he's doing

so much for your career.'' The words were said with a sneer.

She shoved her fists to her waist. ''And what's that supposed to mean?''

His eyes narrowed as he stared at her. ''You're a darn good actress, Alexis. You had both me and Bryan fooled. I guess it's understandable how you could charm a ten-year-old kid, but me, a grown man...'' He shook his head in disgust. ''You fooled me into believing you cared about us.''

''I haven't been acting around you!'' Tears threatened, but she blinked them away. ''I care about both of you. Why are you talking this way?''

''And what way is that?'' he asked with a deceptive calmness.

''Like you hate me.'' The words came out in a whisper.

''No, I don't hate you, Alexis. I'm just not going to let you use either me or my son again.''

She felt as if she had stepped into quicksand. The future that only a few days ago looked so rosy was murky and slippery. What was happening? Where had things gone so wrong? ''I don't understand.'' She looked to him for an explanation.

''I know why you've been pretending to be Bryan's friend.''

''I'm not pretending!'' she denied vehemently. ''I love Bryan. He's like a—''

''Like what, Alexis? A son?'' he interrupted. ''That's what you planned all along, wasn't it? To treat him like a son so you could show the world that you really are the motherly type.''

"No, it isn't, and I don't know why you would even think such a thing.'' Realization suddenly dawned. The night Ray had been at her place he had mentioned meeting Judd. Had they discussed the photo of Bryan that had been in the paper?

"I heard the truth with my own ears,'' he told her, a steeliness in his voice.

She straightened, determined to hold her ground. "It's not the truth, and I don't know what Ray said to you, but you've obviously misunderstood.''

"I misunderstood?'' he asked in exaggerated disbelief. "I was in the courtyard when you and your publicist chose to discuss the subject of your career.'' He gave her a word-for-word replay of the conversation.

Alexis was stunned. "But there was more to that conversation. You can't possibly believe I would even consider doing such a thing as using Bryan for publicity!'' The quicksand continued to pull her.

"I saw the photograph of you and Bryan in the paper.'' His eyes burned with anger.

"And you put two and two together and came up with six.'' She spat the words at him. "Without hearing my response to Ray's comments, without asking me what it meant, without coming to me and discussing your concern that Bryan was photographed without your consent. Well, for your information,

Judd, I didn't want that picture taken and I sure didn't want it splattered across the newspapers.''

She could see he didn't believe her.

"My work makes me susceptible to all sorts of invasions of privacy—that's part of my job, and I accept it, but I don't have to like it and I certainly don't encourage it," she said ardently.

"But you're more than willing to use it if it will get you a juicy role, isn't that right?"

She could only stare at him in disbelief. "I thought you understood this crazy business I'm in, but I can see I was wrong. You're no different than the people who buy those gossip papers and believe every word in them is true."

"And what am I supposed to believe?"

For one moment she thought she saw pain in those dark brown eyes, but it disappeared when Bryan's voice called, "Dad?"

"I've got to go. Bryan needs me," he said, his face impassive.

"Tell him I said hello." She choked back the emotion in her throat. "You must know that I care about him and that I want him to get well soon."

"Is that the real Alexis talking or the make-believe mom?"

The quicksand had swallowed her. She didn't answer, but turned and walked away. The last thing she heard was the slamming of his door.

CHAPTER TEN

"I WISH I could go see Alexis," Bryan told his father as they ate breakfast one morning.

Judd sighed. "I thought we had agreed it would be better if you didn't go over there anymore."

"But I miss her, Dad."

The misery on his son's face made Judd's heart ache. "She's a busy lady," he said between bites of toast that tasted like cardboard.

"You always say that about her when you don't want me to see her," he chastised his father. "Why don't you like her anymore, Dad?"

"It's not a question of me not liking her, Bryan," Judd answered honestly. It would have been much easier to shut Alexis out of his life if he didn't have any feelings for her.

But he did. And that's why he couldn't forget her. Nor could he forget that she had never really cared for them, had simply seen them as a vehicle to further her career.

"Then why can't I go see her?" Bryan demanded.

"Because you can't," Judd snapped impatiently. A glance at the clock told him they needed to get moving. "You're going to miss the school bus if you don't hurry.'' He pushed himself away from the table and carried his dishes to the sink.

"What about the present I made for Alexis?'' Bryan asked. ''I have to give it to her before she leaves.''

"Leaves?'' That brought Judd to a halt.

"As soon as she tapes the last episode of 'Two Plus Two' she's going back to Colorado.''

A hollow feeling settled in Judd's stomach. Alexis was leaving? She hadn't mentioned anything about going away to him. She hadn't cared about him. Surely if she had, she would have told him her plans.

"We'll talk about this tonight, all right, Bry?'' He handed his son a napkin. ''You have a milk mustache.''

Bryan wiped his face, then scrambled to get his backpack. His last words to his father before he raced out the door were, ''My teacher says when you have a fight with someone you need to both sit down and calmly talk it over. Can't you do that with Alexis?''

If only it were that simple, Judd thought as he watched his son hurry to the bus stop. As he drove to work, his mind was occupied with thoughts of Alexis. She'd been the one who allowed herself to be photographed with his child. How could she have not known what was going on? He justified his mistrust and anger all the way to the office, marched in and slammed the door behind him.

Frankie was in her usual place behind the desk reading one of her ever-present tabloids. ''I brought a cake this morning. German chocolate. It's in the kitchen. Help yourself.'' There was a smear of coconut frosting next to her lip.

Judd held up the mirror Frankie always kept on her desk, and she whisked away the frosting. ''Did you know there was a three-headed cow born in India? Weird, huh? It says here—''

''Frankie, I don't want to hear any of that. Have we had any calls in the last twelve hours?''

''Three. All airlifts from local hospitals to bigger medical centers. And all three have been completed successfully.''

''Great.'' Judd always liked to hear that no patient had died en route to treatment. He felt a personal stake in getting everyone transported as quickly and as safely as possible. That, perhaps, was why his company had such a good reputation.

''Hey, boss, are you going to purchase that helicopter?''

The one he had test-flown with Alexis. The memory of how he had enjoyed showing her the city at night flashed in his mind, reminding him of how much he enjoyed being with her. There would be no more romantic flights, no kisses.

''Boss?''

''What is it?'' he asked shortly, causing Frankie's eyes to widen. He was never sharp with her—even when she deserved it.

''I just wanted to know if you're going to get that new helicopter.'' She eyed him curiously. ''Is something wrong?'' Frankie was never one to be intimidated by the men she worked with. That was both her curse and her charm.

He rubbed a hand across the back of his neck. "I'm just in a lousy mood."

"Uh-oh. I sense there's a woman involved. Does this have something to do with the lovely TV star you're dating?"

"*Was* dating," he corrected her.

Frankie's face fell. "It's over? But she's so sweet and she was so good with Bryan!"

Judd chuckled sardonically. "It was all an act."

"How can you say that?"

"Because I have proof. You know that photo of her and Bryan at the zoo? Well, that was all set up so she could improve her image. She wanted to look like the motherly type she plays on TV so she could further her film career."

"Are you saying she was only being nice to you and Bryan because she wanted a part in a movie?" Frankie asked, her mouth agape. When he nodded soberly she stated passionately, "Well, I don't believe that for one minute!"

Judd sighed. "It's true. I heard her publicist gloating over the success of that one photo. It was a setup from the beginning—befriend a motherless boy and get the press to believe she is every bit as nice as the character she plays on TV. For all I know there could be photos of my son splashed across every tabloid in the country, and for one reason only—Alexis Gordon is ambitious.''

"Wait a minute. Aren't you the one who's always telling me we shouldn't pay any attention to all this stuff in the paper?''

"Yes, but that photo is different. It's *my* son.'' His fists tightened as he said, "She befriended him for one reason only—to use him.''

"Are you sure about that? I mean, if she were only using Bryan for publicity, wouldn't she have taken the photograph the first couple of times they were together and then dumped him?''

The phone rang. Judd answered it in his office, leaving Frankie to return to her perusal of the tabloid. She had only turned a couple of pages when her mouth dropped open in horror.

"Oh, my!''

As Judd hung up the phone, he couldn't help but notice she was speechless. "What is it?'' he asked, walking over to her.

She handed the paper to Judd. On the page, in living, if somewhat grainy, color was his son Bryan leaving the hospital after his skating accident. Alexis was a couple of steps behind him. Judd was at his side, a fierce scowl on his face. A stark white cast on Bryan's wrist and bandages on his legs and arms made Bryan look critically injured. There was a frown on his face as if he were holding a grudge. The headline read, Alexis Gordon Nearly Kills Lover's Son in Fit of Anger.

Judd's face tightened as he stared at the page. "This is ridiculous!" he roared. "Bryan broke his wrist skating and Alexis is not my lover! How can they print such lies? Don't they care who they hurt?"

Frankie could only shake her head in regret. "Obviously not."

"Do you realize the power these papers have over people's lives?" Judd asked, dropping into a chair. "It's not just the celebrities and innocent kids they photograph, but anyone who reads the stories in hopes of living vicariously through their heroes and idols. People are willing to accept any scrap of information the publisher wants to give them, whether it be true or not."

"I never thought of it that way," Frankie admitted, then dumped her stack of tabloids into the trash. "I don't need to read that garbage."

Judd looked at the photo again and felt sick to his stomach. The photographer had deliberately chosen a snapshot with Bryan brooding and Alexis trailing him in order to manipulate the headline. If truth were known, Bryan was pouting because Judd had refused to let him ride with Alexis. Another snapshot could have shown him smiling at her as she comforted him.

For he had smiled at her often that day—as he had every time he had been with her. Bryan loved Alexis, and she loved him.

It was a realization that hit Judd like a ton of bricks. She had gone out of her way to be nice to his son, to make his life a little less lonely. And all Judd had done was to doubt her sincerity and accuse her of orchestrating publicity.

Judd walked into his office and sank down in his chair. He'd been so hard on Alexis, so willing to believe the worst of her. When she tried to explain about her publicist, he had refused to listen. She could have easily been the victim of an ambitious man, just as she'd been the victim of an ambitious photographer.

One thing he did know. She had not hurt Bryan in a fit of anger, as the tabloid suggested. And it might be that she hadn't used his son to improve her image, either. How could he be sure? Until he found the answer, he was not going to have any peace of mind.

"Are you mad at my dad?" Bryan asked Alexis as he fed Iggy bits of lettuce.

"No. Why do you ask?"

"Because...you know," he said shyly.

"Your father and I aren't seeing each other anymore."

"Yeah. And he says I shouldn't come over here because you're busy."

"I do work a lot, but I like it when you visit me," Alexis answered honestly.

"Then it's my dad you're mad at," he concluded, making Iggy reach for his next treat. The little jaws snapped ferociously, startling Bryan. "Whoa! I guess I'd better not tease him."

"Bryan, just because your dad and I may have had

a difference of opinion doesn't mean you and I can't be friends," she said carefully.

"My teacher says that everyone should always be able to work things out. That's the 'adult' way to do it."

"There are some issues that even the most adult adults have trouble with, Bryan," she said gently, loving the little boy more every time she saw him. It hurt to think the day might come when Bryan would no longer be in her life.

Iggy had demolished the lettuce, and Bryan lifted him into his living quarters for a nap. "Well, I wish you would try, because my dad's been really grouchy ever since you had your difference of opinion. Even Mrs. Wahlstrom thinks he's acting like a bear with a sore paw."

His words brought little comfort to Alexis. Maybe Judd was as miserable as she was, but it didn't change the fact that he didn't trust her. In his eyes she was a phony and a woman to avoid.

She tried to be as cheerful as she could, but the ache in her heart grew until she thought it would fill her chest and smother her. As much as she enjoyed Bryan's company, it was a relief to see him go home, for she couldn't look at him and not see his father.

Several days later Judd walked into Lifeline Air Service and plopped a newspaper on Frankie's desk. "Read that."

She pushed it aside. "Oh, no. I'm through with those tabloid papers."

He shoved it at her, his finger on a column circled in red. "No, you must read this."

"Correction. Contrary to what was reported in last week's paper, Alexis Gordon was not responsible for Bryan Shepard's broken arm. The boy fell while skating, and it was thanks to Ms. Gordon that he received such prompt medical attention," Frankie read aloud. "You got them to print a retraction?" She stared at Judd with admiration.

"My lawyer did. He did some snooping around, and as it turns out, one of the editors at that paper had a good reason to listen to my side of the story."

Seeing Frankie's astonishment, he explained. "You see, a couple of months ago I transported this guy's wife in an emergency. When he found out it was me and my son in the photograph, he was willing to set the record straight."

"Way to go, boss!" Frankie congratulated him. "Do you think Alexis has seen this?"

Before he could answer, the phone rang. As Frankie took down the message, her eyes grew wide.

"Emergency call from the television studio at…"

As she repeated the address, Judd felt a sinking in the pit of his stomach. That was Alexis's studio.

"It's on the set of 'Two Plus Two.'" Frankie confirmed his suspicions. "A bank of lights broke from the ceiling, and an actress standing underneath has been injured. The paramedics suspect a spinal cord injury.''

"I'm on my way."

"Judd, should you be the one to go? Just it case it's—''

He didn't allow Frankie to finish the sentence. He was outside and in the air as fast as he could move. His hands were shaking, his mind racing.

Alexis. He knew it had to be her. "Two Plus Two" was a four-person show—mother, father and the twins. He'd watched it so seldom that he had no idea if there were guest stars. He'd never seen one.

A possible spinal cord injury. Of course, it was standard procedure to make sure no possibility was overlooked. It didn't mean there *was* a spinal cord injury. In his mind, he could see an injured Alexis, her healthy, athletic body crushed beneath an imaginary track of lights. A cold shudder bolted down his spine.

Fear threatened to control his adrenaline. He couldn't lose her now, not when he had finally come to his senses and was about to set things straight between them.

As the studio came into sight, he felt fear as if it were a vise tightening around his heart. Relying on the skills and self-control that had earned him the reputation as a top-notch pilot, he landed the helicopter on the pavement.

A paramedic greeted him. "Well, that was fast. Good thing, too. She's in a lot of pain. Come on.''

"Who's hurt? Is it Alexis Gordon?" he asked, but the paramedic was running ahead of Judd, leading the way through a maze of corridors and camera equipment.

When they arrived at the set, it looked as though a bomb had crashed through the room. Huge banks of lights were lying in a tumble, along with pieces of ceiling tile. There was a gaping hole in the ceiling. Pieces of debris had been shoved aside to create a path to where a woman lay on a stretcher. Judd's first glimpse was of long, honey blond hair cascading over the side.

It was Alexis. His heart seemed to fall to the soles of his feet. He'd never told her he loved her, and now this. He'd never even admitted to himself it was possible to love again until it came crashing down upon him just like the ceiling had done on this set. What if she died? What if he were too late?

"Judd, are you all right? You look terrible." A familiar and concerned voice came from behind him.

He spun around to see Alexis, her face pale, her eyes wide.

"You're all right!" He grabbed her in his arms and held her so tightly that she finally squeaked.

"I will be if you don't crush any of my bones."

He let her go and studied her face with an intensity that radiated from every part of him. "When the call came in, all they said was that a woman had been injured—" He broke off, too choked with emotion to speak.

"And you thought it was me?" she finished for him, her voice gentle.

He nodded, then hugged her close for a second time. "Thank God it wasn't."

She eased away from him. "It could very well have been. Shandra is my stand-in. They were doing some blocking and I was in makeup when I heard this terrible crash. We ran out to find her buried under the wreckage." Her voice faltered.

"Okay, Judd. We're ready!" one of the paramedics called.

Judd said quickly, "I have to go, but I need to talk to you. When can I see you?"

"I'll be home this afternoon. Nobody's going to be able to work after this, not until we know how Shandra is doing."

"I'll be there as soon as I can." He took her face between his hands and gave her a long, hard kiss. Then he was gone.

He stayed at the hospital only long enough to see the injured woman transported into safe hands. Then he was in the helicopter and on his way to the airstrip. When he landed, he was relieved to see that no other choppers were missing. That meant no other calls.

Frankie was waiting for him at the door. "Was it Alexis? Is she all right?"

"Alexis is fine. The woman injured was her stand-in. It's a miracle it wasn't Alexis, though. A few minutes later and they would have changed places." The thought was enough to produce a shiver in Judd.

Frankie leaned against the wall. "That must have been scary."

Judd didn't bother to comment on her understatement. "Listen, I can't be here this afternoon. Have you got anyone you can call to fill in for me?"

"I can try, but you'll probably have to pay time and a half."

There was no price Judd wouldn't have paid to be with Alexis. "No problem. Just do it."

A half an hour later he was still at the airstrip. "I can't believe you can't find anyone," Judd moaned, feeling as if he was getting closer to losing his sanity with each passing minute. He needed to be with Alexis.

When it became obvious he wasn't going to be able to leave, he called her. He felt his heart pounding like a trip-hammer in his chest as he waited for her to answer the phone.

"Judd, hi," she said quietly.

He could imagine how fragile she must look. "I'm stuck at the office. Have you heard how Shandra is?"

"No. I've been waiting. My imagination has been going wild."

"No wonder. It was a serious accident, but that doesn't always mean people have serious injuries." He knew how shallow his words sounded.

When the phone clicked, indicating call waiting, Alexis asked him to hold the line. A few minutes later she returned. "That was someone from the hospital," she explained.

"And?" he gently prompted.

"Shandra's going to be all right." She gave a huge sigh of relief. "Broken bones but nothing serious. Some ribs are fractured, as well as a couple of bones in her arm, but the doctors say she'll heal without any aftereffects. Her neck and spine are fine."

"Then the prognosis is good," Judd commented.

"Uh-huh. One thing she does have is a concussion, and apparently she can't remember the accident, which is probably a blessing. She's in intensive care and will be for a few days."

There was so much Judd wanted to say, but they were things that couldn't be said over the phone. "We have a lot to be grateful for. I thought my heart was going to stop in my chest when I saw that honey blond hair streaming off the stretcher."

"I'm fine."

Her voice was distant. Judd wondered if she was angry with him. "You're sure you're okay?"

"Uh-huh."

There was dead air, then Judd said, "Alexis, we need to talk."

"About what, Judd?"

"About all that stuff with the tabloids."

She sighed. "I think you've said quite a bit about them already."

He could tell from the hostility in her voice that this was not an apology that could come via the telephone. "I need to see you, Alexis."

"Why? So you can tell me how phony I am? Look, Judd, I've got to go. There's somebody at my door."

And before he could utter one more word she had said goodbye and clicked off.

Alexis didn't know why she had been so nasty to Judd on the phone. Maybe the accident had made her edgy. She hadn't accomplished much of anything the rest of the day. Now here it was, nine o'clock at night, and she was as restless as she had been when she left the set.

Not that she hadn't tried all sorts of remedies. A hot bath with candles burning and a glass of wine. Her favorite music. Her favorite author. Her favorite food. There was nothing on television she could stand to watch. Everything seemed shallow and boring. To occupy herself, she decided to clean her closet. She did it every once in a while, usually when she'd reached a new point in her life and realized the clothing she owned was for a woman who didn't exist anymore. "Ritual shedding," she called it. She was certainly no longer the woman she'd been a few months ago.

The glittery, low-cut dresses went first. She was a homebody, somebody's sister, somebody's friend. Not a dress-up doll. Not any longer. Not for her agent or her publicist. Not even for her career.

The soft cottony dresses that made her feel cool and comfortable stayed, as did several professional-looking suits that always made her feel less like a starlet and more like a businessperson. The casual clothes stayed, everything that spoke of comfort and practicality. Low-cut anything found its way into a discard pile, as did uncomfortable shoes and ridiculous undergarments that were built like suspension bridges and made to reshape her already perfectly proportioned figure.

When she was done, there were gaping holes between the garments left, and the giveaway piles on her bed were heaping. She would give everything to Shandra when she got out of the hospital. They were exactly the same size, and Shandra was paid a pittance. The clothes would be a real boost for her—something fun to look forward to wearing. And Shandra would be doing her a huge favor if she'd take them.

Feeling slightly better, Alexis headed for her makeup counter. It was filled with pots and potions, brushes and sponges, foundations and lipsticks to match every possible garment in her closet.

Since I don't have the clothes anymore, I won't need these. Alexis picked up the garbage can and began to fling things into it until she had only the bare minimum of makeup left. That she put into a small basket and set inside the closet.

She was feeling better, more like herself—the woman she'd been when she came to California. She'd bought into the glitz and glamour then—but not anymore. She wanted to be real. If a movie part came along, she would grab it in a heartbeat. She could read scripts from Colorado and have a normal life at least part of the time.

There were stacks of clothing, overflowing garbage bags and various cast-offs all over the living room when the doorbell rang. Alexis was wearing a wildly colored striped jumpsuit and a pair of unmatched shoes, something she'd tried on while cleaning out the closet. She considered ignoring the bell. Still, it could be Jenny Williams. Sometimes she stopped by. She opened the door.

There stood Judd holding a pie plate containing the most pitiful looking pie she had ever seen. The crust edge looked as though it had been pounded into submission with the tongs of a broken fork. The top was lumpy, reminding Alexis of a child hiding under the bed covers. The edges looked singed and the middle suspiciously underdone.

"What's this?" She wanted to hate him, but he was too darn good-looking and he had a sparkle in his eye that set her pulse fluttering. He was in stocking feet and wore faded jeans and a pale green sweatshirt.

"Humble pie." He held it out. "For you, from me."

"You've got that right," she said, eyeing the lumpy dessert. "It's the most pitiful—I mean humble—pie I've ever seen. What am I supposed to do with it?"

"Accept it and then have some with me. That's why I'm here—to apologize and eat my humble pie." Judd looked genuinely chagrined. "I was a jerk of the first degree. I'm sorry. I know now that there was no way you could have controlled those photos in the tabloids. I've been with you and haven't noticed photographers anywhere. I was wrong to accuse you of using my son to further your career.''

"They have telephoto lenses the length of small cars,'' Alexis said sharply. "They can be a block away and still get pictures.''

"I know that now.'' Judd looked worriedly at the pie. "So will you accept my apology and my pie or not?''

"Did you make it yourself?'' Alexis asked.

"Doesn't it look like it?

She laughed. "I think Bryan and Andy might have done a better job.''

"The crust is from scratch. Mrs. Wahlstrom's recipe. And I made the filling all by myself.'' Judd was edging his way inside.

"Is it a humble *apple* pie? I suppose I could take a taste and decide.''

Taking that for a yes, Judd moved into the room and shut the door. For the first time he looked around. "What's going on here? A rummage sale? And what, exactly, are you wearing?'' He was staring at her mismatched shoes.

"I was cleaning closets. I do that sometimes when I'm making big changes in my life. You know, out with the old, in with the new.''

He set the pie on the table. "Am I the old?''

"Do you want to be?''

For an answer he pulled her into his arms and kissed her. It was the kind of kiss that left little doubt as to his feelings for her. When it was over, they were both breathing heavily.

"I guess you can be the new," she said, then carried the pie into the kitchen. He followed her.

"Bryan told me you're leaving for Colorado." His gaze held hers.

"I want to visit my family."

"And then?"

"And then I'd like to make a movie."

"So they'll let you do that in the summer and then come back to 'Two Plus Two'?"

"Yes, but the truth is I'd like to quit the show. My contract is under negotiation."

She cut into the pie and frowned. "It's hard. I don't think I can cut it."

"You don't have to. Just scrape off the top crust."

She stared at him. What was he doing, giving her a pie that was as hard as rocks? She did as he urged and peeled back the layer of crust only to discover the pie was full of rocks! She looked at him for an explanation.

"I feel as dumb as those rocks." He tugged sheepishly on his ear. "In my heart I knew you wouldn't have arranged for someone to take that photograph of Bryan at the zoo, but..."

"But?"

"But I was seeing red because of Bryan. And at

the time I didn't realize how out of control those tabloids are with their lies. I'm sorry, Alexis.''

"They truly are out of control. You must have seen the photo taken outside the hospital."

He nodded soberly. "There's something else in that pie."

She moved the rocks around until she found the newspaper clipping. She read it, then stared at him with misty eyes. "Thank you."

"It was the least I could do. I only wish I could have gotten them to put it in block letters across the front page, but at least it's there."

She smiled gratefully.

"There's another reason I filled the pie with rocks. They have significance."

"You mean because of what happened with Bryan?" She gave him another skeptical look.

"Yes. You see, I think that was the day I fell in love with you."

Her look of confusion changed to one of disbelief.

"It's true, Alexis. I love you. The way you walk, the way you smile, the way you are with Bryan. I love everything about you, and I don't want to live without you in my life," he said tenderly.

She shoved her hands around his neck and pulled him into her arms. "I love you, too, Judd." Then she covered his mouth with hers in a deep kiss that told him just how sincere she was in her declaration.

When they finally came up for air, she asked, "What about my occupation?"

"It has its advantages and disadvantages, just as mine does," he answered.

"What if I want to move to Colorado?"

He grinned. "Have you forgotten? I'm a pilot. The distance between California and Colorado is not that great." He trailed kisses across her cheek until once more he found her lips. "Actually, I've been thinking about selling Lifeline Flying Service. The hours are too long for someone who wants to spend more time with his son and wife."

"Wife? You're thinking of getting married?"

"I'm hoping I can convince a certain make-believe mom to be a real wife and mother." This time the trail of kisses crossed her neck.

Alexis leaned her head back to give him access and said, "Can anyone audition for this role or has someone already got the part?"

He nibbled on her ear and said, "It's all yours for the taking."

She smiled and said, "I accept."

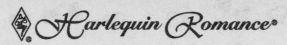
Harlequin Romance®

We're proud to announce the "birth" of a brand-new series full of babies, bachelors and happy-ever-afters: **Daddy Boom**. Meet gorgeous heroes who are about to discover that there's a first time for everything—even fatherhood!

Starting in February 1999 we'll be bringing you one **Daddy Boom** title every other month.

February 1999: **BRANNIGAN'S BABY**
by Grace Green

April 1999: **DADDY AND DAUGHTERS**
by Barbara McMahon

We'll also be bringing you deliciously cute **Daddy Boom** books by Lucy Gordon, Kate Denton, Leigh Michaels and a special Christmas story from Emma Richmond.

Who says bachelors and babies don't mix?

Available wherever Harlequin books are sold.

HARLEQUIN®
Makes any time special™

Sexy, desirable and...a daddy?

THE AUSTRALIANS

Stories of romance Australian-style, guaranteed to fulfill that sense of adventure!

This February 1999 look for

Baby Down Under

by **Ann Charlton**

Riley Templeton was a hotshot Queensland lawyer with a reputation for ruthlessness and a weakness for curvaceous blondes. Alexandra Page was everything that Riley *wasn't* looking for in a woman, but when she finds a baby on her doorstep that leads her to the dashing lawyer, he begins to see the virtues of brunettes—and babies!

The Wonder from Down Under: where spirited women win the hearts of Australia's most independent men!

Available February 1999
at your favorite retail outlet.

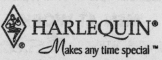

MEN at WORK

All work and no play?
Not these men!

January 1999
SOMETHING WORTH KEEPING by Kathleen Eagle
He worked with iron and steel, and was as wild as the mustangs that were his passion. She was a high-class horse trainer from the East. Was her gentle touch enough to tame his unruly heart?

February 1999
HANDSOME DEVIL by Joan Hohl
His roguish good looks and intelligence drew women like magnets, but Luke Branson was having too much fun to marry again. Then Selena McInnes strolled before him and turned his life upside down!

March 1999
STARK LIGHTNING by Elaine Barbieri
The boss's daughter was ornery, stubborn and off-limits for cowboy Branch Walker! But Valentine was also nearly impossible to resist. Could they negotiate a truce...or a surrender?

Available at your favorite retail outlet!

MEN AT WORK™

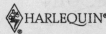 

Coming Next Month

#3539 BACHELOR AVAILABLE! Ruth Jean Dale

Cody James was tall, sexy and handsome—he took Emily Kirkwood's breath away. Too bad that Emily hadn't joined the Yellow Rose Matchmakers to find a man but to write a Valentine's story on... well...how to get a man. Only, Cody *was* available...and perhaps what this story needed was a little in-depth research!

Texas Grooms Wanted! *Only cowboys need apply!*

#3540 BOARDROOM PROPOSAL Margaret Way

It's the job of her dreams, but can Eve Copeland believe that she won it fairly and squarely? Her new boss, after all, has a secret he'd go to great lengths to conceal....

#3541 HER HUSBAND-TO-BE Leigh Michaels

Deke Oliver was convinced Danielle was trying to manipulate him into marriage—just because they'd jointly inherited a property...and were forced to live together under the same roof! But Deke wasn't husband material, and Danielle simply *had* to convince him that she wasn't dreaming of wedding bells!

#3542 BRANNIGAN'S BABY Grace Green

When Luke Brannigan asked Whitney for help, she was torn. On the one hand, she wanted to get as far away as possible from this annoyingly gorgeous man, who insisted on flirting with her. On the other, how could she refuse to help when Luke was obviously struggling to bring up his adorable baby son?

Daddy Boom—*Who says bachelors and babies don't mix?*